ZAFIRA

The Guzun Bratva Book 5

Linzi Basset

Zafira

A Dark Mafia Novel

By

Linzi Basset

Copyright © 2024 Linzi Basset - All rights reserved.

Linzi Basset

ZAFIRA: THE GUZUN BRATVA #5
Copyright © 2024
Edited: Sandy Ebel
Proofreaders: Marie Vayer, Charlotte Strickland, Rhea Foxx.
Publisher & Cover Design: Linzi Basset – Version 5/22/2024
ISBN:

Warning: the unauthorized reproduction or distribution of this copyrighted work is illegal. Criminal copyright infringement, including infringement without monetary gain, is investigated by the FBI and is punishable by up to 5 years in prison and a fine of $250,000.

Linzi Basset has asserted her rights under the Copyright, Designs, and Patents Act 1988 to be identified as the author of this work. All rights reserved. This copy is intended for the original purchaser of this eBook only. No part of this eBook may be reproduced, scanned, or distributed in any manner whatsoever without prior written permission from the author, except in the case of brief quotations embodied in critical articles and reviews.

This book is a work of fiction. The names, characters, places, and incidents are products of the writer's imagination or have been used fictitiously and are not to be construed as real. Any resemblance to persons, living or dead, actual events, locales, business establishments, or organizations is entirely coincidental.

Warning: This book contains sexually explicit scenes and adult language and may be considered offensive to some readers. This book is for sale to adults only, as defined by the laws of the country in which you made your purchase.

Disclaimer: Neither the publisher nor the author will be responsible for any loss, harm, injury, or death resulting from the use of the information contained in this book.

Zafira

Contents

Author's Note	7
Prologue	11
Chapter One	31
Chapter Two	45
Chapter Three	59
Chapter Four	73
Chapter Five	87
Chapter Six	103
Chapter Seven	115
Chapter Eight	127
Chapter Nine	143
Chapter Ten	157
Chapter Eleven	167
Chapter Twelve	177
Chapter Thirteen	193
Chapter Fourteen	205
Chapter Fifteen	221
Chapter Sixteen	235
Chapter Seventeen	249
Chapter Eighteen	261
Chapter Nineteen	273
Chapter Twenty	285

Chapter Twenty-One	295
Chapter Twenty-Two	305
Chapter Twenty-Three	315
Excerpt: Devious Demand	328
Books by Linzi Basset	341
About the Author	347
Stalk Linzi Basset	349

Author's Note

Dear Reader,

The Guzun family is wrought with enigmatic members. Some were taken into the heart of the Matriarch, only to betray the trust she had in them. This is Zafira's story... the woman of steel who was the silent backbone of the family and the Bratva organization.

Blurb

The conclusion to this riveting dark Mafia series.

Zafira Guzun

The Guzun Matriarch, or *Comare*, as everyone in the Bratva world called me. A name I earned as the wife of one of the most respected Bratva leaders ever. After his death, I stepped back, preferring to leave the hard decisions to my children... or so everyone thought.

Betrayal is a hard pill to swallow. This time, it turned sideways in my throat. Now, I'm being suffocated by those I loved and trusted unconditionally. No more... It is time they suffered the consequences.

Bogdan Rusu
The *ubiytsa smerti* or the death slayer, as everyone in the Bratva called me. A moniker I earned as the advisor to the Pakhan of the Guzun Bratva. I'm respected because I'm a nice guy... but I'm feared more because I have no mercy.

Keeping Zafira Guzun safe has been my priority since her husband passed away. It hasn't been easy, especially since she meant more to me than being my boss. She was my heart... except she didn't trust me, and that hurt... deeply.

In the end, only one thing mattered...

Who needs to forgive, and who needs to make amends... or will pride and hard-headedness be their undoing?

Note: Although the blurb is in 1st POV, the book is written in 3rd POV.

This series must be read in order because if you thought you knew how it's going to end... you're wrong.

I enjoyed weaving these intricate tales of violence, woven with love, regret, hate, and misunderstanding. This is the end of their respective journeys, closing all the loopholes and showing us that love always finds a way to conquer... even if it takes over four decades.

Warm regards,
Linzi Basset

Linzi Basset

Zafira

Prologue

The year 1979... The Cathedral of Christ the Saviour on the wedding day of Zafira Solovyov...

"*Ostanavlivat'sya*! Stop complaining. It is done, Zafira. Today is your wedding day. You will not dishonor this *sem'ya*, me, or your *otets* with your continued whining about true love."

Zafira hardly heard her mother as she paced anxiously in the luxurious waiting room adjacent to the grand cathedral. The white lace wedding dress trailed behind her. The room was lavishly decorated for the special occasion. Beautiful bouquets of red roses and white lilies were arranged in crystal vases on mahogany tables. Silk drapes framed the large arched windows overlooking the Moscow cityscape.

Zafira was oblivious to the opulent surroundings as she wrung her hands while pacing across the plush Persian rug. Her heart felt heavy at the distress of being forced into a marriage not of her choosing.

"*Mamochka*, please!" Turning to face her stern-looking mother, she pleaded her case. "You always said I would be allowed to choose my own husband. This isn't my choice!" She struggled to maintain her composure and blinked back tears that threatened to spill down her cheeks.

Viktor Guzun was indeed a very attractive man—strong, powerful, and skilled at seducing women. At first, he had made Zafira's heart flutter nervously whenever he entered a room. But that initial infatuation had faded quickly, replaced by an all-consuming love for his best friend, Bogdan Rusu.

Just one look from Bogdan—with his rough around-the-edges attitude, rugged features, and muscular frame—took Zafira's breath away.

Sheer anguish at being forced to marry another tore through her soul. How she longed to run away with Bogdan against all obligations to her family. Her azure eyes pleaded with her mother to understand.

Over time, her feelings for him had grown steadily deeper until she treasured their secret love fiercely in her heart. She had been careful to hide it from everyone, scared of the consequences if it was discovered.

And her fears hadn't been for naught. The day her father informed her that he and Viktor's father had come to an agreement that she would marry him, she refused. It was also the day she had made the biggest judgment error of her lifetime. She had told her father of her love for Bogdan. The conversation she had with him echoed in her mind.

"Bogdan Rusu isn't in our class, Zafira. He will never be able to offer you the kind of life you are used to. Most definitely not the life of luxury and wealth Viktor Guzun can."

"Money isn't everything and I have more than enough of my own, or did you forget my inheritance from grandmother?"

"I didn't, but perhaps you should ask yourself if Rusu would be as interested in you if you weren't a rich woman?"

"Bogdan isn't like that!"

"Isn't he? Well, let's test that theory, shall we?"

"He isn't like that! Nothing you do will ever make me believe it." Zafira stormed off with tears of anger and despair running over her cheeks. Knowing her father, he wouldn't back down. He had made a decision about her future, and come hell or high water, he would make it happen.

She was yanked back to the present as the heavy footsteps of her father came thundering down the hallway. Each step echoed off the vaulted ceilings of the lavish waiting area. Zafira's heartbeat quickened as her chest tightened with anxiety. She knew the confrontation coming would not be pleasant.

The elaborately carved mahogany door swept open as Anatoly Solovyov stormed into the room. His hulking frame seemed to take up the entire doorway, with his broad shoulders nearly scraping the ornate moldings. He had always been an imposing man, but today, his sheer size and presence were downright intimidating.

Zafira shrank back and recoiled from the shadow cast across the room as her father blocked the light. His expensive Italian leather shoes clicked sharply on the inlaid marble floors when he strode toward her with his eyebrows drawn together in irritation.

"What is the hold-up?" His barrel-chested voice boomed through the open space. "Everyone is waiting, and the priest is becoming impatient."

Summoning her courage, Zafira lifted her chin. "I'm not marrying Viktor Guzun, *Otets*. I don't love him, and I—"

"Don't tell me you're still hung up on that worthless Rusu?" Anatoly interrupted with a derisive snort. He moved even closer. Zafira forced herself not to shrink away as he loomed over her. Her defiance presented itself in her balling fists.

"I warned you he's a gold digger." A smug, self-satisfied smirk spread across her father's broad face. Relishing the moment, he slowly took out his checkbook. "And now,"—he paused for dramatic effect—"I have the proof."

With a flourish, he shoved a check stub under Zafira's nose. With her heart sinking, she scanned the amount. It had far more zeros than any honorable man would accept. She could hardly swallow past the lump in her throat as she blinked back hot tears of dismay.

It couldn't be real. Bogdan wouldn't betray her, not after his passionate words of love and devotion. But the evidence was right there in black and white. Her romantic dreams crumbled to dust, and the world fell away beneath her feet. Utter despair flooded through Zafira. She felt adrift and heartbroken.

"I don't believe it." Her voice sounded foreign to her ears. Grief stricken, she stumbled to a chair and sat down.

"*Nyet!* Get up! You're wrinkling your dress."

"*K chertu plat'ye!*" Zafira sneered. Her voice rose as she shouted again, "Fuck the dress, *Mama!* I don't give a shit about wrinkles. You don't even care that *Papa* is ruining my life!"

Zafira

"Oh, no, dear daughter," Agata Solovyov said with a gentle voice as she sat down next to Zafira and took her trembling hands in hers. "At first, I was against what your *papa* was going to do, but when he showed me proof that Bogdan had taken the money... This is for the best, Zafira. At least with Viktor, you are assured of a man who loves you, and once you forget about that heartless hustler, you'll see a bright future ahead with Viktor."

"You saw that Bogdan took the money?" Zafira's voice cracked as she felt her entire life crumble to pieces.

"Yes, *moya doch'*, the check was cleared by the bank. I'm so sorry for your heartache, but that man isn't worth your tears."

"You will see, Zafira," her father snickered. "He's Viktor's best man at the wedding, but he won't attend. He's gone off with the money."

Zafira's heart died a little at that moment. Bogdan Rusu was the only man she had ever wanted and had fallen in love with. It wasn't just a first love scoffed; it was a once-in-a-lifetime true love denied to grow to full potential.

"Very well, *Papa*. If Bogdan isn't at the chapel standing next to Viktor as his best man, I will marry him."

"And will you do everything in your power to make the marriage a success and make us proud?"

"I will come to love him, *Papa*. I will give him a family and be the best supportive Bratva wife ever born."

"I believe you, daughter." Anatoly narrowed his eyes. "Men like Bogdan always come back. If he does, however far in the future, will you remember the vows you're about to make to Viktor and forsake whatever feelings you still have for Bogdan?"

"If Bogdan truly sold our love for a couple of million rubles, he's not worth a moment of my time, *Papa*. I will honor my vows, and I will come to love my husband."

One year later... The IK-3 penal colony, Kharp in the Yamalo-Nenets region, 1200 miles northeast of Moscow...

Zafira

"This is it, Prisoner R666. The Day of the Damned." An evil cackle sprang from the warden's lips. He was in his element, and although the prisoner's only response was a stoic stare, it was obvious that he relished every moment of the full control he had over the worthless vermin—as he referred to the inmates—who were incarcerated in the prison. "Win this fight, and you will walk out of here a free man."

Bogdan Rusu didn't bother responding. He had learned early on to keep his mouth shut. No one listened, and the only benefit earned from defiance was time in the darkest solitude hellhole on earth.

That he was in prison for no reason and without charges didn't matter. All that did was that his size and strength had made the whiny little shit of a warden thousands of rubles every week since the first day he had woken up in a cell a year ago—on the very day the woman he loved got married to his best friend… And he hadn't been there to put a stop to it.

The bargain the warden had struck with him was the only thing Bogdan had been clinging to, however, he realized over time Boris Balakirev was a bald-faced liar. Bogdan wasn't naive. Boris had no intention of letting the man who was his money pit walk out of prison.

The Day of the Damned was an annual event where the champions of prison colonies across Russia fought like animals for survival in a cage... to the death. Only the strongest and bravest survived, and it came with a very hefty cash purse to the winning prison. With Bogdan as their champion, it was the first year the IK-3 penal colony stood a chance. Of course, the prison wouldn't benefit one ruble from that money. It would all go straight into Boris Balakirev's back pocket.

Penal colonies were descendants of Soviet-era gulags, the notorious Stalin-era labor camps where thousands of Russians lost their lives. In Kharp, Navalny temperatures were as low as -40°C. There was little light for six months of the year, and in summer, mosquitoes and midges became an inmate's worst enemies.

Bogdan was incarcerated in the exceptional regime. A detention that was reserved for the most dangerous prisoners, those sentenced to life imprisonment or those whose death sentence had been commuted to life imprisonment. Since Bogdan had committed no crime and was illegally detained, he only had one assumption to make.

Konstantin Guzun, Viktor's father, had found out about him and Zafira. Bogdan knew him well enough to realize it would be his way of making sure the future he had set out for his eldest son would come to fruition. To him, it didn't matter that Zafira didn't love Viktor... But as with everything in his entire life... what Viktor wanted, Viktor got.

Konstantin wanted the picture-perfect family for Viktor, which included a wife who was well-known and came from a feared Bratva family. Zafira was perfect in every way.

What hurt more than losing the woman he loved was the agony of not knowing whether his best friend, since they were in pre-school, had betrayed him as well. Was it only Konstantin and Anatoly Solovyov involved in his illegal incarceration? Or did Viktor play a part as well?

Thinking of the humiliation and anger that had been at war inside himself the day Anatoly gave him the check and told him to stay away from Zafira caused a wave of despair to wash over him. He had been fighting the darkness from rearing its head for an entire year, knowing if he allowed it to come to light, he might never find a way to leave this hellhole.

Bogdan had stared at the amount boldly scribbled on the check, more money than many families would ever earn in a lifetime. For him, it was a pittance to the wealth he had at his disposal. No one, not even Viktor and the Guzun family, knew where Bogdan originated from. To be honest, neither had he... until his twenty-first birthday, when a legal team had come for him.

His mother had been banned from her family when she married Bogdan's father. The day she died of a heart attack was the day his grandfather, the Grand Duke Matvey Mikhailovich Romanov, claimed his only living family. Upon his death, four months before Bogdan was jailed, as his grandson, he inherited everything, even the coveted title of

Grand Duke. None of which mattered to him since he had lost the only person he ever wanted to share his life story with.

It ended now... here today. He had wallowed in self-pity long enough. Today was the day he took back his life. It was time Zafira found out the truth. He hadn't walked out of her life with her father's money. In fact, the check was still at the family castle in Moscow—kept as a reminder to never lose all sense of humanity in the vile world of the Bratva and become like Konstantin Guzun and Anatoly Solovyov.

He could only hope and pray Zafira hadn't fallen prey to the same fate most of the Bratva Pakhans' wives did—and became cold and filled with emptiness.

"*YA govoryu s toboy!* Hey, R666! I'm talking to you," Boris sneered. He quickly stepped back as Bogdan turned his head and looked at him. Everyone knew better than to invade the giant man's personal space. "Don't give me that look," Boris defended himself. "You spaced out, and the fights are about to start. We need to take our place next to the cage." He snickered as he rubbed his hands together in expectation. "I suspect the matches are going to be vicious and short. You might end up in the cage much quicker than anticipated."

"I'm walking out of this colony today, Warden Balakirev."

Boris avoided his gaze, but his head bobbed up and down. "Of course. Of course. I promised, didn't I?"

"You're not hearing me, Warden." Bogdan's voice turned ominous. "I'm walking out of the colony today. It's your choice whether I leave with you by my side or with your head separated from your body tucked under my arm."

Balakirev turned as white as a sheet. "Th-There's no need to threaten me, R666. I made a promise. I will keep my word."

"See that you do because nothing, not even a bullet in the chest, will stop me from leaving here today."

"Win this contest, and you're a free man."

"I better be, Warden... or you'll be a dead man."

Zafira

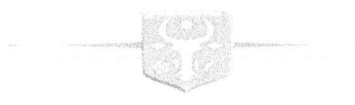

Two weeks later... Ferma La Guzun, the residence of Viktor and Zafira Guzun, nestled on the banks of the Dniester River, Dubasari, Moldova...

Bogdan's footsteps slowed as he approached the grand farmhouse where he had spent so much time with his best friend. Viktor had insisted he move in there after they finished college, and until his incarceration, this had been his home for the past five years. Years where he had secured his mark as a mobster in the Guzun Mafia as one of the youngest and best assassins on the circuit.

"How quickly time changes," he muttered as he looked around and took in the lush gardens surrounding the property. Vibrant flowers bloomed in meticulously tended beds while weeping willows trailed long branches into the river. The wraparound porch was painted a pristine white, which contrasted beautifully with the dark wood accents and green shuttered windows.

As he stepped onto the porch, a movement near the willow trees caught his eye. There, sitting on a quilt spread out on the grass, was Zafira. The sunlight filtered through the willow branches above her, illuminating her in an ethereal glow. She was even more beautiful than he remembered. With dull eyes, he noticed her holding a sleeping infant, bundled snugly in a soft blanket.

Bogdan's breath caught in his throat as Zafira gazed down lovingly at the baby. Her face was more radiant than he had ever seen it. At that moment, Viktor emerged from the gardens and made his way over to his wife and child. As he sat down beside them, Zafira looked up at her husband adoringly. Viktor smiled and placed a tender kiss on her forehead before stroking the baby's cheek.

"I'm too late." The loving scene hit Bogdan like a punch to the gut. In that instant, he knew he had lost her. While he had been fighting for his life, biding his time to get out of that hellhole, he had lost her. Yes, he had known she would marry Viktor, but he had hoped she would've kept the love she had for him in her heart. Instead, it was evident that she had fallen deeply in love with her husband; otherwise, she would never have started a family with him. The life they shared together now was one he could never be part of.

Bogdan's shoulders slumped in defeat as his heart fractured in anguish. There was no place for him in her world anymore. The pain of loss and regret threatened to overwhelm him. Forcing himself to turn away, Bogdan walked off the porch.

"Bogdan! My God! It's you!" Viktor's elated shout stopped him in his tracks.

For long moments, he didn't move as he gathered the strength to face the happy couple.

"Get over here, you big lout! Come and meet Arian… my son."

"*Isus Hristos*, I don't know if I have the strength for this," he muttered as he turned around and slowly approached them. Viktor met him halfway and hugged him fiercely.

"Where the hell have you been? I've been worried sick. We've looked everywhere for you. How could you just disappear like that, Bogdan? Fuck that, I don't care. I'm just happy you're back and here to share the joy of my firstborn with us."

Bogdan stopped and stared at the infant, whose azure eyes sparkled as he unblinkingly returned the big man's gaze. At that moment, a bond formed between giant and baby. One that showed in his eyes as he lifted them to look at Zafira.

"Well, look who decided to come back." The scorn in Zafira's voice was thinly veiled, but he detected the hurt it attempted to mask from him.

"Believe me, Zafira, if I had a choice, I would never have left."

"You're your own man, Bogdan. We don't own you. No one does. You can come and go as you please." She smiled brightly. "Come... meet our son."

At that moment, as he stared into her eyes, he identified the silent, unconscious plea in the depths of her gaze. The decision to stay and keep her safe was an easy one. He might have lost her love, but his own heart still cherished the feelings for her deep inside. As long as those embers burned, he would stay by her side and protect her from harm. Kneeling beside her, his fingers trembled visibly as he reached out to take the baby boy's small hand.

"Pleased to meet you... Arian Guzun."

Linzi Basset

Zafira

Chapter One

Current day, Tampa Bay at Temptation Club, Largo, Florida, U.S.A....

"Please, Master Slayer, I can't hold it anymore. I need to come! Please... fuck me."

"We've hardly begun, subbie. I'm far from ready to fuck you." The loud cracking sound of the flogger's leather strips on skin married with the cries and strikes echoing throughout the torture chamber of the exclusive BDSM club. "I need much more to get me high on endorphins before I will indulge in the need for sexual release. For now, I crave that euphoric high only a good, sadistic flogging offers me."

Walking closer, he pressed his large body against the trembling form of the female submissive tied up on the St. Andrew's Cross.

"You claimed to be a masochist when we discussed the scene. It seems that was a lie. Should I find a replacement, subbie? One who can take what I dish out?"

It had taken Master Slayer, aka Bogdan Rusu, years to learn how to channel Dom space on demand. Once he established the mechanism to achieve that coveted feeling by relaxing and focusing on the moment rather than chasing the altered state, he found it easy. Dom space was similar to what subspace was to submissives, except a Dominant had to stay in control during a scene since they had to remain sensitive to safe words and other signs that their partners were not comfortable or enjoying themselves.

However, to Bogdan, there was a kind of letting go that divorced him from the outside world and offered an escape from the stormy sea of emotions churning within while channeling his focus toward the submissive in a hyper-intense way.

Zafira

It was the only means, during a narrow window, that he could lose track of time and the world around him while in Dom space. Where it felt like he was high on drugs with amplified sensations and a feeling as if he was out of his body. His sense of intuition was enhanced as he made a stronger, more intimate connection with the masochistic partners he scened with.

For Bogdan, it offered a brief yet precious escape from the hellish recollections that clung to him daily like ghosts hungry for his anguish. A reprieve from remembering that he had wasted his entire life loving a woman who, in the end, proved she never loved him.

Tonight, he couldn't reach that much-needed space, no matter how hard he tried. His mind inevitably drifted back to that fateful day one year ago when he had confronted the only woman who he had loved his entire adult life, Zafira Guzun—a decision that haunted his dreams to this day. His chest tightened as he recalled how foolishly he had clung to the slender hope that she still harbored some residual affection for him. He had laid his soul bare, only to have her cruelly reject him with callous indifference.

"Vanya is wrong. You just can't move on, can you? All these years..." He shook his head, and for the first time since he'd met her, he allowed a sadness to crawl over his face. "I wasted thirty years of my life hoping, missing out on companionship, love, having children because I was waiting... such a fucking waste."

"Stop talking in riddles, Rusu. Say what you came to say, then leave. I have things to do, and you're wasting my time... No! Let me go! What are you doing?"

Zafira gasped for breath as suddenly, he was in front of her with one of his huge paws curled around her throat as he pushed her back against the windowpane. Tension etched every line of his powerful frame as his hold tightened as he forced her onto her toes.

"Bogdan, stop," she choked out, tears forming in her eyes. It was the fear that was painted over her face that doused his anger. His gaze softened, *although his hold didn't. With his thumb, he traced the fullness of her bottom lip as a sadness engulfed him when the truth finally hit home.*

"So beautiful… and yet so cold."

"B-Bogdan… please."

"I'm done, Zafira. We end this now, one way or another."

"End what?" *she croaked, desperately clawing at his hand.*

Disappointment was chiseled over his face at her response. A gulf of misunderstanding yawned wide between them.

"You just can't admit how you…" *He sighed.* "So be it. I'm done defending myself, and I'm done being your emotional punching bag. You want me out of your life, Zafira? Then so be it… I'm gone."

With a muffled oath and a final sweep of a rough fingertip over her lip, he released her and walked out with long, measured steps.

"No, Master Slayer! Please don't find another sub. I can take it. I swear I can." The pleading wail of the submissive yanked him back to the present.

Bogdan shifted restlessly as he fisted his hands until his knuckles turned white. His jaw was tight as he forced the surging emotions back behind the steel wall he had erected around his heart. He had no choice since, no matter how much time had passed, the searing pain remained as raw and fresh as an open wound.

God! I have been such a fool. He berated himself once more for wasting his entire life loving someone who never reciprocated.

Zafira hadn't called out to stop him when he had left. Not a whimper, a whisper... no sound at all. She had watched him walk out of her life and accepted it.

That—more than the empty, lonely months since or the wasted years spent loving her—hurt most of all.

The electric light sconces cast dancing shadows across the room but brought no warmth to the cold emptiness devouring Bogdan from within. He yearned for the sweet oblivion of Dom space, to lose himself in an intimate scene where he was desired and in control. But the bitter memories of

Zafira

Zafira's betrayal refused to loosen their vice-like grip on his mind, keeping his emotions churning like a volcano ready to erupt.

Enough! I've had enough. It's time to move on, forget about her, and find another to fill my heart.

The thought came from nowhere, but he latched onto it like a starving leech. He needed to make a change quickly before the last of the little humanity he had left disappeared. He longed to feel human and filled with warmth from within again.

"I changed my mind." The growl emitting from his chest, albeit gruff like the beast he was known as in the hallowed hallways of the club, was flat and emotionless. With quick, economic movements, he untied the trembling sub and picked her up. "Let's go fuck."

Master Slayer was known by the submissives as a Dom who didn't play games. He spoke his mind and took what he was after, but only from those willing to play at his level. At times, with his piercing glare and cocksure attitude, some called him rude and obnoxious, but since his sexual exploits were on every woman's lips who were regulars at the club, no one cared. As long as they got to be one of the lucky ones, ending up with him in the private rooms upstairs.

Casey, the submissive, scrambled back on the bed as he flung her down. His one eyebrow crawled upward in a mocking salute as he unfastened his belt with slow, deliberate intent.

"Changed your mind, subbie?"

"No. It's just... you seem angry, Master Slayer. Don't get me wrong, I love rough sex as much as the next one, but you look ready to rip me to shreds with your bare hands."

Bogdan looked down at his hands, realizing they were curled into vicious-looking claws. No wonder the sub was having second thoughts. He might have allowed the sadist in him free rein the past year, but he always made a point of giving as much pleasure as pain. Yes, he fucked rough, but only if the sub was up for it, and he was assured she achieved a level of euphoria that surpassed any pain she might experience should he lose control. Not that he had to date, but like with everything in life, unforeseen shit happened.

Relaxing his muscles, he continued to undress. His eyes followed the valleys of her full figure. She was a favorite with the sadists at the club since she knew how to tease and unlock the beasts inside them without screaming and crying when the devil was unleashed—exactly what he needed tonight. He offered her a brief smile.

"You can relax, subbie. The sadist has gone to sleep… for now." Naked, he kneeled on the bed, untouched by the way her eyes hungrily devoured his solid, muscled frame. Big, bulky, and strong, he represented a human beast, which was why he was called Master Slayer at the club—except no one here knew about his past, they had no idea how appropriate the name was to him as a man. "Get on all fours with your ass in the air. Keep your head down at all times. I suggest you grab hold of the slats of the headboard. Otherwise, I might drive you through the wall."

Bogdan never had sex in the missionary position. He didn't want to see the woman's face he was fucking. All he needed was the warmth of a hot pussy clamping around his cock as he drove himself to release. Yes, it sounded heartless, but it was exactly how he had been able to survive all these years—having sex with other women while he remembered the few times he had the privilege of being with the one he loved. It was a poor substitute but the only way he could cope.

The brush of his hand over her left buttock cheek drew a surprised gasp from her.

Crack! Crack!

"Fuuuck!" she screamed as he smacked the shit out of her bottom. The two ruthless slaps immediately left bright red imprints on her white skin.

"I warned you to keep your head down. Look up again, and I walk away. Is that understood?"

"Yes, Master Slayer." She whimpered as he scraped his nail over the abused part of her skin, igniting more pain to writhe through her. His dick responded with an excited twitch.

"Good girl." A low, rumbling chuckle bounced off the walls as he swiped a finger through the slit between her labia. "I see this little pussy truly loves pain. Such a delightful aroma wafting through my nostrils, subbie. Indeed, an invitation I can't refuse." With his cock encased in a condom, he settled behind her and positioned the blunt tip of his cockhead at the entrance of her channel. With one finger toggling her clit and the other hand tugging and pinching her nipples, he pushed inside her body a half-an-inch. She wiggled her hips, moaning enticingly. "Are you ready, subbie?"

"Oh, fuck yes, Master Slayer."

"Better hold on to those slats then, little whore, because this is going to be a fucking rough ride."

"May I come, Sir?" The question was mumbled as she pressed her head into the pillow while clutching tightly at the bedposts.

"Come at will, subbie." The laugh that followed sounded like Hades incarnate. "This isn't going to be over quickly."

"Then what are you waiting for, Master Slayer?" she taunted him as she moved her hips back, forcing his cock deeper. "Fuck me silly, Sir."

A deep growl reverberated through the room as the next moment, he shoved his cock so hard into her, the bed slammed against the wall.

"Jesus Christ," she screamed as his hard-driven thrusts pushed her already primed body to climax within seconds.

"Better keep breathing, subbie. That was only the beginning."

Being tall and powerful, Bogdan pounding into her lifted her knees clear off the bed. Her screams of pleasure soon turned to pitiful cries of overindulgence as his huge cock kept driving into her mercilessly, forcing one climax after the other from her.

By the time he ejaculated, she was a limbless mess, weakly holding onto the slats, her body sleek with sweat as she gasped in labored breaths.

"Go take a shower. I'm going to get us something to eat. You need to re-energize for round two." He smiled at her disbelieving look. "I find I enjoy the sound of your squishing cunt, subbie. I'll be availing myself of its wetness until the sun rises."

Zafira

"Holy shit," she wailed as she slipped from the bed and crawled toward the ensuite bathroom since her legs refused to cooperate.

Linzi Basset

Chapter Two

"About time you finished. I was worried we might have to camp out here in the hallway the entire night."

Vanya Guzun's voice tiptoed a path of forgotten affection through his mind as he walked out of the room. Ignoring the couple he spotted in his peripheral vision, he kept walking.

"Please, Bogdan. It's time for you to come home."

The words didn't stop him in his tracks. It was the voice of a forlorn little girl begging to be picked up and carried on his broad shoulders. A lost little girl reaching out for the love of a father... a role he had fulfilled since Viktor had died.

"We miss you, and we need you. *I* need you."

Bogdan shook his head as he attempted to resist the pull her pleading voice represented. He refused to turn around and face them. Vanya wasn't the crying type, but he could hear her voice thickening with suppressed tears.

"Arian needs you, Bogdan. More than anyone. You have always been his rock, ever since he was a baby. You were his hero, the one he looked up to. To him... to all of us, it's as if we lost a father... again. Please, come home with us."

"I am home, Vanya." From the flat tones in his voice, the message was crystal clear. He wasn't interested.

"No, you're not. You don't fit in this country, Bogdan. You are a true Romanian. It's in your blood. You know it as well as we do."

"This is my home now. I have a business, and I have built a new life." He still hadn't turned to face them.

"A business? A new life? Don't make me laugh. You are no fisherman, Bogdan. You're Bratva. That is another fact you can't run away from."

"Correction, Vanya." Bogdan turned. None of the emotions at seeing her lovely face showed on his. Vanya, all of the Guzun siblings, really, were like his own children. He had missed her the most since she had been like an added attachment to his leg whenever he was around her growing up. "I own the most successful fishing trawling business on the Miami coastline. I supply fish and seafood statewide." His smile was sardonic. "Even to Moldova."

"But are you happy, Bogdan?"

He suppressed a smile at her tenaciousness. Vanya had come here with a goal, and it was more than evident she wasn't leaving until she achieved it.

"I am content."

"See! You're not happy," she cried out, elated.

"Leave it, Vanya. Happiness is overrated, and only you yourself are responsible for your own. Over the past year, I've often asked myself what it means to be happy and—"

"It's when—"

Bogdan's raised hand cut her excited interruption short.

"Sonja Lyubomirsky, a professor of psychology at the University of California, defines happiness as 'the experience of joy, contentment, or positive well-being, combined with a sense that one's life is good, meaningful, and worthwhile.'" His expression turned grim. "The reality is, going back to Moldova isn't going to bring me any of those. I've been fooling myself for years. I've never been truly happy, especially over there.

"No, Vanya. I appreciate you coming out here, but I am right where I belong now. There's nothing for me in Moldova." A humorless cackle escaped his lips. "I find I rather prefer being a fish mobster than a human one. At least there are no broken families left behind when I chop off a fish's head. Well... some would debate that, but you get my drift."

In the world of the Bratva, Bogdan was known as *ubiytsa smerti*, the death slayer, a moniker he had earned early on as the advisor to the Pakhan of the Guzun Bratva. He was respected because he was truly a nice man with a dry sense of humor.

However, he was feared more because, as an assassin, he showed no mercy to those who opposed or hurt any of the Guzun Bratva family.

Strangely, since it had become a way of life for him most of his adult life, it was this aspect that he hadn't missed over the past year. In fact, he reveled in not having to kill or look over his shoulder for the next stupidly brave one, wanting the accolade of beating the *ubiytsa smerti*.

"If you don't want to go back to Moldova, then at least come and live with us in Andrei's castle in Russia. Just come home with us." Vanya caught his hands as she entreated earnestly, "We need you."

"I'm not going, Vanya. Accept it."

With a heavy sigh, Vanya turned to Andrei. "You have to tell him. It's the only way." Her eyes locked on Bogdan as she gestured to the big man who had been watching him with burning eyes. Andrei always had a way of shrinking the biggest man to the size of an ant. Where Bogdan was the slayer of men, Andrei's gaze was the slayer of confidence. "He needs you the most." Her hand curled around her belly. Bogdan's eyes narrowed as, for the first time ever, he noticed a tender smile of expectation cross the fearless woman's face. "As does your... grandson."

"My what?" Bogdan's fists landed low on his hips. "What nonsense are you spouting, Vanya?"

"You are my father, Bogdan." Andrei spoke up for the first time. "Remember, I went to the homeland statistics department and the lab that did the DNA test years ago when my uncle claimed Viktor was my father?" His eyes darkened. "I found out they did four different tests. Only one sample showed a ninety-eight percent match to my DNA. I personally had it verified again after Janos died.

"Vanya is right. You are about to become a grandfather. I need my father in my life, especially now that I'm about to become one. I never had a real father. The one who claimed me as his son was a shit face, Uncle Janos was worse, and Viktor... well, we both know how he was. I need an example to guide me when my son is born. You were there for the Guzun family when their father died. I need you in my life now." Andrei walked closer. "I finally realized why I was always so drawn to you. Why I felt a deep connection from the first day we met. My soul knew who you were. Please, come home with us... *Tată*."

"I can't be... I've never... I believed Janos was lying about Dimitri Balan not being your father at the time purely to hurt Zafira. I didn't have sex with Nikita that..." Bogdan's words became strangled in his throat as he cast his mind back to Viktor's bachelor's party. "I haven't thought of that night for so long because I was having the worst time of my life. Celebrating the joy of my best friend getting married while my heart was crushed about losing the woman I loved. I chose to lock it from my mind because it was after that night, and upon our return home, that I was thrown in jail."

"In jail?" Vanya's brow furrowed ominously. "Why don't we know about that?"

Bogdan sighed. "Apart from Viktor, his father, and Zafira's father, no one knows I was incarcerated for a year for no reason. When I returned and found your mother happy with a little baby boy as a sign of her love for her husband, I chose not to tell her."

Leaning against the balustrade, Bogdan's eyes turned smokey as he watched the people having fun below.

"Everyone seems so happy and carefree," he muttered. "I forgot what that feels like."

"You can be happy, *Tată*."

His body shuddered in reaction when Andrei laid a hand on his shoulder. A gesture he had performed many times over the years, but this time, it felt different. It shook Bogdan to the core... knowing it was his son, his own flesh and blood, comforting him.

"With us and our son... Boian Bogdan... Rusu."

"Rusu?" Bogdan's voice cracked as he stared at Andrei. That they were naming their son after his father and him made his heart swell to bursting point. A happiness he was unfamiliar with filled his soul as for the first time, he identified similarities in Andrei's features and his own. He was happy to notice that Andrei had invested in plastic surgery, and only a thin scar remained under his eye from the harrowing shot that had almost cost him his life.

"Now that I know who I am, Vanya and I want to start a new beginning for our children, so we chose to do so with my real surname," Andrei continued. "I can now finally be who I was born to be, and it's a tradition we want our descendants to continue. That's why we changed our surname to Rusu and decided to name our firstborn after my blood grandfather and you… my birth father.

"I don't know what to say… or feel. All of this is so sudden and…" He turned away as, for the first time in his adult life, he struggled to keep his emotions under control. "I was so focused on keeping Viktor from fucking Nikita that I forgot that I ended up with her." The hand he ran over his face trembled. "I did have sex with your mother that night. In fact, I was the last one who did. I kept her busy so she would leave Viktor alone." His breath escaped in a broken exhale. "Jesus Christ, is it real, Andrei? Are you truly my son?"

"Yes, Bogdan Rusu, you are my birth father." Andrei's smile silenced all doubts Bogdan might have mustered up. "I will show you the DNA results to set your mind at ease."

"That's not necessary. I believe you." He shook his head. "It was my one biggest regret in my life," he mused out loud. "That I was so true in heart and mind to Zafira that I never had a family, a child of my own. Now... after all these years..." His eyes filled with tears. "It can't be true. Life can't be that filled with bliss and cruelty at the same time."

"And yet it is, *Tată*," Vanya said as she hugged him fiercely. "I can't be happier that you are now my father for real."

"Who are you, and what have you done with my Vanya?" Bogdan said as he pushed her away and frowned at her. "You even look different," he said in a gentler voice when her eyes watered up. "Don't you dare start crying because then I'll know you're an alien who invaded my princess' body."

Bogdan's eyes widened as she did just that and with a sob, flung herself into his arms.

"*Destul*, Andrei! What is happening to her?"

"You have a very short memory, *Tată*. Did you forget how Zafira became when she was pregnant? The steely, strong woman broke down and burst into tears at the smallest provocation. Crumbling under a mere frown from you." He gestured at Vanya. "She's like her mother in that aspect. I've seen a totally different side to her, but I doubt it's something I would dare remind her of once our little boy is born and she's back to her old self."

"I forgot about that," Bogdan murmured as he returned Vanya's hug. "There, there, *malen'kaya printsessa. Blyad'*," he growled as his gentleness sparked a fresh wail from her. "She's more like Zafira than I realized. She, too, sobbed when I used to call her pet names at times like this."

"Here." Andrei handed him a handkerchief. "I suggest you start carrying a stack with you in the future. Otherwise, you'll be walking around with wet patches on your shirt every day."

"I'm not that bad," Vanya protested but took the proffered piece of cotton to wipe the tears from her face. Her smile lit up the dimness of the hallway. "So, *Tată*, are you coming home with us? Once we get there, we're going to start decorating the nursery. I'm sorry, love." She hugged Andrei. "But I don't trust your DIY or painting skills."

"No need to apologize, *moye serdtse*," he said with a broad smile. "I can build a house, but little bits and pieces... not for me."

"Where is home, Vanya?" Bogdan had to ask. He was overwrought with pride and joy at the news, but living a couple of miles from Zafira... he wasn't ready for that, especially knowing she had no feelings left for him.

"Chiverevo, in Russia. We have demolished Janos' house and rebuilt the castle Andrei always dreamed of having."

"It's not a castle, love. It's a stately mansion," Andrei interjected.

"It's a castle," Vanya reiterated with finality. "He specifically designed it so that you have your own wing. It's connected to the house but completely separate at the same time. You have a private swimming pool, two spare bedrooms, and your own front and back doors, but you can also use the interleading ones to the rest of the castle."

"House," Andrei said.

"Castle," she continued unperturbed. "So, since there's no reason you can think of that I will accept, *Tatǎ*, you might as well give in, say goodbye to the little chit in there, and go home to pack."

The word *tatǎ* kept milling through Bogdan's mind every time one of them used it. Father... a word he had never expected to be called. It rocked him to the depths of his soul. For the first time in his life, he experienced a spark of what happiness felt like. He clung to it like a drowning sailor, afraid if he didn't, he would lose any chance of finding a speckle of it ever again.

"Well, since you put it that way..."

Linzi Basset

Chapter Three

U Holubů restaurant, Bílovec, Czechia...

"Chert voz'mi! You were right."

Zafira Guzun, the Guzun family Matriarch, or *Comare*, as she was still called after all these years by the majority of Bratva groups in the EU, stared with a deep frown at the live CCTV footage on the security monitors. Even after Viktor's death, when she withdrew from the Business and allowed her children to rule, she was respected and feared by those who had intimate knowledge of the power she had over the once-powerful Pakhan.

Except she never truly stepped back. She merely retreated into the shadows from where she continued to build a network of loyal followers who preferred her way of handling matters that threatened the well-being of the Guzun Bratva Group.

Neither her kids nor any of the Guzun Bratva associates knew about her covert life—except Antonio and one other person. The one man she had trusted with her life, only to find out, in the end, that he, too, had betrayed her. Even though he had sworn unconditional fealty to her, without her asking for it, she now realized that he had been very selective in what that care and protection entailed. That he still chose to shield Viktor's reputation from her hurt the most. He had kept his best friend fucking a woman at his bachelor's party from her. How many others were there that Bogdan Rusu had kept from her?

Her chest closed up. With fingers circling her throat, she gently massaged it as it felt like something was squeezing her esophagus closed, slowly suffocating her by those memories—of the ultimate betrayal by the only man she had ever truly loved and trusted unconditionally.

Zafira

Enough, Zafira! No more. He's out of your life for good. He chose to walk away rather than fight for a love that has been dormant for years.

The sharp voice echoing in her mind snapped her out of her momentary lapse into the emotional darkness that had wrapped itself around her from the day Bogdan had walked out of her life. The days of empathy and being nice were over. All those who believed she and her family could be walked over were about to suffer the consequences of their ignorance.

For Zafira Guzun was as fierce and fearsome as Viktor Guzun had been—even more so since her children's lives were threatened.

"Of course, I am." The deep voice of Antonio Baritva rumbled through the small room. They were secure in the office building across the street from the restaurant. Her new bodyguard and advisor had set up the surveillance there. A necessary precaution that Bogdan had always insisted on when she ventured out alone to functions or meetings with any Bratva or syndicate leader. Somehow, Antonio knew every trick Bogdan had implemented to keep her safe, even though he wasn't around to train his successor.

No, the bastard just turned around and walked out of my life!

Her body turned cold as the echo of the last words he had ever said to her raced through her mind.

"So be it. I'm done defending myself, and I'm done being your emotional punching bag. You want me out of your life, Zafira? Then so be it... I'm gone."

Why couldn't she forget? She was supposed to have moved on. A year, twelve long months, and still, his words hounded her every day when life quieted down, and she settled into sleep. Much-needed rest that she never got since the hours were filled with memories, needs, and hidden desires she had been too proud to voice in the years since Viktor's death.

"*Comare?*" Antonio's concerned voice yanked her back to the present predicament. "Are you okay? You look pale?"

Zafira

"I'm fine." Other than with Bogdan, she had yet to share her emotions or inner fears with Antonio. He was trustworthy and loyal to a T, but as the saying went, once bitten, twice shy. Zafira would never open up to any man like she used to with Bogdan.

Her eyes sharpened on the screen as she watched the footage of the Czech police raiding the birthday party held for one of the deputies of the Solntveso Bratva. Two hundred partygoers were detained, which, as was usual at these affairs, included dozens of prostitutes. The event was held in the restaurant U Holubů, owned by Seymon Mochilevich, aka Uncle Seva, aka the Brainy Pakhan—also a longtime friend of Zafira. Seymon was a well-known Russian mobster who was regarded as one of the most powerful gangsters in the world.

"Who else was aware that the party was a cover for the meeting with me?" Zafira was supposed to meet with Seymon Mochilevich and Artem Melnyk, head of the Solntvesoka Bratva. Foot tapping on the floor, she leaned forward with her fists on the desk. "What the fuck is going on, Antonio? I thought you did a due diligence check before I accepted the invitation to come here rather than meeting in Moldova."

"I did, *Comare*. Nothing indicated that the police or anyone else knew you were attending the party. Besides, they have nothing on you, so even—"

"There's always a reason for a raid, Antonio. You know as well as I do that Luciano Maranzano escaped, and he's out there somewhere with a burning desire to kill every last Guzun member of my family. He's secured one of the widest networks across the globe he can now tap into for support. Someone like Artem Melnyk could be easily swayed to turn on one of his own."

"Which is why I pulled you out of the restaurant the moment I got word that the police were on their way. According to my source, they had been tipped off that the Solntveso group intended to execute Mochilevich at the party over a disputed payment of five million dollars."

"Mogilevic hasn't arrived yet," Zafira said thoughtfully. "Why do you think that is?"

"Could be that he'd been warned by a senior figure in the Czech police. You know he has a couple of them working with the Russian Bratva."

"Or he could be siding with Maranzano, and the raid was used as a cover to assassinate me."

"I thought you were friends since school?" Antonio watched her intently. "Why would he betray such a friendship?"

"Friendship means shit in the criminal world, Antonio. I'm sure you've learned at least that over the years with us." She sat down and crossed her legs with feminine grace. The dark blue silk of her evening gown rustled quietly in the room. "It's become common knowledge that since Viktor's death, someone has quietly built a highly structured criminal organization. Although only a selected few know I am the leader who is referred to as the Shadow Don, I don't think Seymon likes that the Shadow Don is now described by agencies in the European Union and United States as the boss of all bosses of Russian Bratva and crime syndicates in the world."

"Of course, a title he coveted. I didn't think about that." Antonio shifted his weight. "It's believed you direct a multibillion-dollar international criminal empire, which is why the Federal Bureau of Investigation describes the Shadow Don as the most powerful and dangerous gangster in the world."

Zafira shrugged. "You know I still operate in the shadows, Antonio, but it's true. I have immense power and reach on a global scale. It took me years and hard work to secure valuable connections to prominent government, military, and law enforcement officials, not to mention powerful politicians around the world. To achieve that in a male-dominated industry wasn't easy. No matter how many fearless female Bratvas there are, women are still not given the time of day."

"Yet your own children nor anyone at the Guzun Bratva know you are the Shadow Don who the FBI accuses of weapons trafficking, contract murders, extortion, drug trafficking, and prostitution on an international scale."

"They're reaching by adding prostitution to the charges. It's the one thing I have no interest in exploring." Zafira shrugged. "My children don't need to know… not yet. Everything I have done over the years has been to protect them. First, from how volatile Viktor had become in the later years, threatening the continuation of the Guzun Bratva, which was hugely financed by my family at the time, and now, to keep them safe from Luciano Maranzano."

"My lips are sealed, *Comare*."

"Except, now it seems one of the trusted few has ratted me out. The question is, just when?"

"How can you be so sure, *Comare*?"

"The only reason Luciano Maranzano would want me dead is because I am the only one standing in his way to achieve his goal to become the supreme boss of all bosses globally."

"But he shot you over a year ago."

"Exactly, Antonio, which tells me whoever has sided with Maranzano has been doing so for years. Yes, he had a mole inside the Guzun Bratva, but he was also always one step ahead of us, the *Novaya*

Volna Group. He knew what we were planning, when we intended to move, the decisions we made. Someone I trusted with my secret is either under the bastard's spell or..." Her brow furrowed ominously.

"Or someone wants the power for himself."

"Exactly." Zafira grinned. "My bet is on the latter. Power and money are a hard taskmaster, and in our business, it's what talks. Of the ones who know who and what I am, any of them would kill to take my place." A delightful laugh escaped her lips. She was clearly unconcerned that someone taking her place meant she would have to die first.

"Oh, to be a fly on the wall when Maranzano realizes he has been played."

"Well, look at that," Antonio folded his arms across his chest. "They're taking Artem Melnyk into custody."

Zafira straightened. "I could use this. Since there is bad blood between Melnyk and Mochilevich, this is the perfect opportunity to cull the weak from the strong." She shook a finger at the screen as if she was scolding the now subdued man being led to a police van. "You never bring out guns at a party where there are innocent women and children, Artem. Let that be a lesson." Her nose inched upward.

"I believe it's time I visited my good old friend, Triska Cermak." She smiled regally as she got up and sauntered toward the door. "Did you know that she and I gave birth at the same time?" she said conversationally as she opened the door and gestured to Antonio to follow her. "She and her husband Marek were on vacation in Moldova when she had complications with her pregnancy, and her daughter was born prematurely."

"Are you saying that you are a personal friend of Marek Cermak, the Prime Minister of the Czech Republic?"

Zafira winked at him. "The one and only, Antonio... the one and only."

"So, Artem Melnyk is going to rot in jail. How does that assure you that he's the real danger and not Seymon Mochilevich?"

"Because, my dear, I am going to make sure the two other people who know my identity as the Shadow Don realize I am the one who had him prosecuted. They'll know none of them will be safe against my wrath. I'm done being used and underestimated. After tonight, not one of them will ever make that mistake again."

After securing Zafira in the backseat, he got into the GMC SUV and started the engine.

"Whereto, *Comare*?"

"I believe it would be wise to stay away from the hotel. No need to play devil's advocate, right? Let's head out of the city. I'm sure we'll find a decent hotel where we can stay overnight. Next week is soon enough to visit my dear friend."

Contrary to her devil-may-care attitude, Zafira felt the band of betrayal once again tightening around her chest. She had given the three men her trust and offered them untold wealth and power as part of the Novaya Volna Group. No matter how much she tried to ignore the feeling, she was hurt and rapidly became angry. Had she been a man, with the equal power and control she already wielded, none of them would have dared to step out of line. One of them did more than that and sided blatantly with the enemy. In the time they had been driving, she had reached the conclusion that it was Artem Melnyk. He was the one who always watched her with a dark glimmer in his eyes. For some reason, she had recently felt a wave of hatred flowing from him. Now, that feeling was what cemented her belief that he had been the one who had given in to the coercion of Luciano Maranzano.

Although there were many variables in what played out tonight, her instinct warned her that she had been the ultimate target.

Zafira Guzun always trusted her instinct.

Linzi Basset

Chapter Four

343 Merirahu Võrgud OÜ, Private Residence Estate, Tallinn, Estonia...

"I'm done for the day, sir." Svetlana Rebane, a born and raised Estonian woman, neatly folded the dust cloth and placed it in the trolley that housed all her cleaning materials. "Do you need my services the rest of the week?"

"*Ei*, Svetlana. But you can come clean and do my washing again on Monday."

"*Muidugi*, sir. I will return on Monday."

Not bothering to respond or walk her to the door, Andrus Klavan returned his steadfast gaze over Tallin Bay. The calmness of the water was in contradiction to the volatile emotions swirling inside him. Life had totally fucked him over. All his dreams of success and grandeur were gone... destroyed by the Guzuns and Andrei Balan or Smirnoff... or whatever the fuck he called himself nowadays.

He'd had a positive outlook his entire adult life. Whatever he wanted, he got. Not because it was given to him but because he refused to let anything, or anyone, stand in his way of getting it—until a year ago... when his entire existence came crashing down on him.

"Have a backup plan, Son, for every backup plan you have."

The voice of his father echoed inside his mind, reminding him that he was better than acting like a broken man crying over spilled milk.

"Except, my fucking backup, backup, backup plan didn't take into account just how far Zafira Guzun's power stretched. I never realized how much control she now had in the criminal world, which surpassed even Andrei's and Arian's combined. Yes, *Padre*. I fucked up. I made one miscalculation, and this is where I ended up."

Andrus, aka Luciano Maranzano, swept a wide arm through the air, indicating, in his opinion, the dismal two-bedroom house he lived in. Gone were the luxury he had basked in his entire life, the money and the strings of people honoring him for the powerful man he was.

Since the Sardinian government had lodged a countrywide manhunt for him, he had been forced to flee Italy. At first, he had laid low and moved between the vast number of properties he owned under the guise of shell companies all across the EU, but the Guzuns had tracked him down every time. They, more than the law, wanted his head. All his allies knew he was being hunted and therefore, refused to offer him a safe haven. The Guzuns were too much of a force to be reckoned with. No one was prepared to anger them by hiding their biggest foe.

"But there is light at the end of the tunnel," he smirked as he lit the one indulgence he still allowed himself, a cigar, the cheap kind, but beggars can't be choosers.

His salvation had come at a time he hadn't expected, nor from a person he could predict would offer him a helping hand.

"Money and power always have the upper hand," he murmured as he dragged the smoke deep into his lungs. "I might not have access to my billions at the moment, but with my new partner's assistance and the cash I stashed away exactly for this kind of unexpected incident, my lifestyle will soon be restored." A low cackle split the air in the room. "As soon as Zafira Guzun is found guilty and put behind bars, the real fun will begin. Then, the odds will once again turn in my favor. I'll be able to leave this shithole country and finally get rid of the rest of the bastard Guzuns... for good this time."

346 Merirahu Võrgud OÜ, Private Residence Estate...

"Well, Svetlana? How is he doing? Anything to report?"

Svetlana Rebane, Luciano's cleaning lady, clamped the phone between her shoulder and chin as she pushed the trolley into the hall closet before walking to the floor-to-ceiling windows of the small

Zafira

great hall area. Changing the call to speakerphone, she removed the gray wig and thick, black-rimmed glasses. She shook loose her long red tresses with the platinum white streaks that made her stand out in a crowd—not only because of the stark contrast but also because she had the clearest azure eyes. It was a rare combination that identified her as someone different since she seemed to have the ability to look right into your soul.

"*Díky bohu,*" she sighed with relief as she stretched the kinks out of her back. "I hate that wig and walking hunched over like a limp dick all day long."

Lithe but strong, she didn't look anything like the middle-aged, crouching woman who went about cleaning houses, well, two houses—the one she resided in and the one Andrus Klavan occupied. She was sent to Estonia with one goal—to keep an eye on him. Make sure he concentrated on achieving the mandate her adopted brother had given him—to assist in ending Zafira Guzun's miserable life.

"Stop complaining, Svetlana. You know as well as I do this needs to be done. We've procrastinated long enough. Now, with Luciano Maranzano desperate for money and the reclaiming of power, we have the perfect tool to get that Guzun bitch out of the way. The gall of the woman to believe strong men, with more money and power than she and all the Guzuns combined, would ever yield to her rule. No, I'll show her how naive she truly is."

"You're a fucking bastard. Don't forget I am also a woman, dear brother. A strong, capable killer who many men fear." Svetlana hated how chauvinistic her brother, all the men in the criminal world really, were.

"No one disputes that, my dear sister, but you at least know your limitations and will never overstep that line. Zafira Guzun is an arrogant, entitled bitch, and I won't stand for it." The sound of a lighter snapping open and closed invited a picture of her brother pacing his study, flicking his priced gold lighter like a scepter. "So, what's Maranzano up to?"

"That's just it. Nothing!" she snapped, not bothering to hide her frustration. "He's still the same. Broods around the house all day long. He hardly goes out for a walk. I'm afraid we might have chosen the wrong assassin for this job. Nothing seems to interest him but wallowing in his own self-pity."

"Then it's high time he snaps out of it. His brilliant plan to have Zafira Guzun locked up during the raid at the U Holubů restaurant failed."

"What do you mean? You confirmed she had arrived in Czechia the day of the party."

"Indeed. So did she at the party, but within minutes, she left with her bodyguard after a heated discussion at the bar. No one overheard what they were talking about, but she didn't return. My sources informed me that they were already in the air, flying back to Moldova, when the armed forces arrived at the restaurant. All the time, effort, and money I put into executing Maranzano's plan was for nothing."

"Not for nothing. Wasn't it there that Artem Melnyk was locked up?"

"*Proboha*, Svetlana! Don't you know anything? Melnyk, as the head of the Solntvesoka Bratva, is invaluable to our plan to have the Guzun, the Red, and the Kolva Bratvas kicked out of the EU Dark Rage Association."

"I know the plan, brother, and I don't appreciate you belittling me. I've said this before, and I will say it again... you are naive if you for one moment believe all the Bratva groups and crime syndicates are going to turn against those three families. They are each a force to be reckoned with on their own. Now that they have combined forces... it's going to take more than Artem Melnyk and the Solntvesoka Bratva to kick them out of the round circle. Arian Guzun has been the chairman for over ten years, and now with Andrei Rusu, the leader of the mightiest Bratva group from Russia, siding with him... it's not going to be easy to sway individual families to turn against them. They fear them too much."

"They will come to fear my power more."

"I have always respected your decisions without asking questions. Now, I believe I need to know. Why do you hate Zafira Guzun so much?"

"Zafira Guzun interfered in our lives at a time when I was ready to take a leap into greatness.

Because of her, I was forced to retreat. Yes, I live a life of luxury and am idolized by all in our country, but I wanted more... more money, more power, and she alone is responsible for changing the course of my life."

"You've said a lot without answering my question, brother."

"That's all you need to know... until such a time that she is no longer a threat to once again disrupt my life and plans of greatness. When she's dead, that's the day I will tell you all."

"I thought you wanted her put in jail? Wasn't that the reason for the raid on the restaurant?"

"Yes, so that she could suffer the most degrading atrocities first. Then I would visit her and watch her face when she realized I was the one who orchestrated the torture she would endure in one of the worst Russian prisons. Then, and only then, would she die."

"Forgive me, brother, but how exactly are you going to achieve that with your master brain assassin wallowing all the way here in Estonia? I don't see any progress being made. To the contrary, it seems destined to fail."

"I agree. Maranzano needs to man up. If he had been present at the restaurant, he could've put a preventive measure in place to keep Zafira there. I'll talk to him. From this point forward, he has to lead every action. I don't need a paper planner. I need action."

"Good. At least that means I'll be able to stop cleaning his fucking toilets."

"Ah, my dear sister, it's good for people in our position to become humble now and then and live the life of the other half."

"Don't let your followers hear you say that."

"I am not an idiot, Svetlana. Now, get ready to move. Find a way to get Maranzano into Moldova without being detected. You leave in the morning."

"Why me? I don't—" But she was talking to herself as her brother had cut the connection. "Fucking asshole," she swore under her breath as she walked toward the ensuite to run a bath. "Always the high and mighty, expecting everyone to bow to his command. I'm so fucking tired of playing second fiddle to him. I am just as capable of running the Chez Bratva, actually more so, than him. I can shoot a feather off a bird in flight. I doubt he can even punch someone in the face, let alone kill another human being."

Between Svetlana and her brother, she was the least emphatic and the most likely to shoot to kill before asking questions. She didn't have a bone of regret in her body for the kills she had under her belt. Some deserved what they got, others... well, they should've known better than to oppose her and interfere with her brother's demands.

"*Bůh zatracenĕ!* I don't want to be the one babysitting Luciano Maranzano," she bleated to the reflection in the mirror. The woman staring back at her could have been beautiful but the harshness of her eyes and her lips permanently pressed into a straight line, she presented a sour and cold expression to the world. If not for the stark contrast of her hair and eyes, no one would bother giving her a second glance.

"That bastard on a bad day is the devil; depressed, he's even more dangerous," she mumbled as she got into the tub. Evil, treacherous, and merciless came to mind. Her brother had no idea what that man was capable of. If he did, he would never expect her to attach herself to him like a proverbial leech.

"How would he? He sits in that luxurious, cozy office of his. He has no idea what goes on in the world out here. But I do... I've seen what he's capable of."

Svetlana shuddered as the vision of the guard, with half his face ripped off by a chain, flashed through her mind. That was when she had first come face to face with Luciano Maranzano... the day he had escaped en route to the prison. When the back doors of the prison van had opened, he had stood there, like a devil on the rampage, holding the bloodied chain, his chest expanding as he watched the man doing the final tango ritual before his body became still. As he lifted his gaze, the pleasure and glee of the kill had shone from his eyes like a beacon on the darkest night.

At that moment, Svetlana knew she was staring Satan in the eye. The evil Lucifer on a rampage to destroy not only those who opposed him but to rip their souls from the depths of their beings.

Svetlana Rebane feared no man… but Luciano Maranzano had become more than a mere human being. He was the devil himself.

Linzi Basset

Zafira

Chapter Five

AVV Airpro, chartered cargo service, based at Chișinău International Airport, Moldova…

The feeling of coming home overwhelmed Bogdan as the door of the Guzun's Bombardier Challenger 600 private jet opened. Although he had been born in Romania, Moldova had been his home and where he had spent most of his life.

Stepping off the jet onto the tarmac, his heart was heavy with a mixture of emotions. The familiar scent of Moldova filled his lungs, a bittersweet reminder of the life he had once known. Memories flooded his mind, each one a poignant reminder of the happiness he'd had a brief taste of and lost. If only he could say he had been happy here. In all honesty, he had never experienced happiness as a grownup. Correction, he had... until he had been thrown in jail to keep him away from Zafira. Upon his return, all hope for finding love and happiness had dissipated. This time was no different.

As his feet touched the ground, a profound sense of emptiness washed over him. This place, once a sanctuary, now felt like a hollow shell, devoid of the warmth and love he had once cherished. Zafira's rejection had left a gaping wound on his soul, and though he had tried to move on, the pain lingered like a persistent specter, haunting his every step.

Bogdan's gaze swept across the familiar landscape, his eyes betraying the turmoil that raged within. The vibrant colors that had once captivated him now appeared muted, as if the world itself had lost its luster. Each breath carried the weight of a thousand regrets, and he found himself longing for the peace that had eluded him for so long.

Clenching his fists, Bogdan fought against the tide of emotions threatening to overwhelm him. He had made his choice, and there was no turning back. Russia beckoned—a new chapter in his life, a fresh start with his son and family. Yet the emptiness in his heart refused to abate, a constant reminder of the love he had lost and the dreams that had shattered.

With a heavy sigh, Bogdan forced himself to move forward, each step a testament to his resilience. The air tasted different, foreign on his lips, as if mocking his attempts to find solace in this place he had once called home. But he knew, deep down, that home was no longer a place but a state of mind—one he had yet to attain.

As he made his way toward the Guzun's private hangar, Bogdan's shoulders slumped ever so slightly, a silent acknowledgment of the weight he carried.

Get a hold of yourself, Rusu. You were gone just over a year. It wasn't a lifetime. Besides, this isn't home anymore.

Moldova was but a fleeting stop on his journey, a reminder of what once was and what could have been. His destiny lay elsewhere, in the embrace of a new life he had yet to fully seize.

You made that choice before you left. Live with it.

"About time you came home." Vadim's voice penetrated his stalemate brain as he entered the vast open space of the hangar. "See, Arian, I told you if there was one person who could get through his thick skull and get him back here, it's our little sis."

"That you did." Arian's voice sounded like it always did—devoid of emotion, but when Bogdan's eyes clashed with his, the elation to see him again shone brightly in their depths.

"I have just set foot on Moldavian soil, and you're pissing me off already," Bogdan's deep voice rumbled from his throat as he struggled to subdue the happiness at seeing the two boys again. "And you wonder why I stayed away so long."

"Bullshit, Bogdan. You're family, and one never forgets that." Vadim drew him into a strong man hug. "You definitely won't. You're our second Dad, you old coot, and you know it."

"You can stop feeding me honey, pup. I'm already here," Bogdan grumbled—as always, he was uncomfortable to be the center of attention and to be faffed over. He loved the Guzun kids; he always had. Apart from Arian, he had been there when they were born, but the life he had lived as a Bratva had taught him to keep his emotions locked away. However, for the first time, it was a struggle to control the lock to the chains that kept his heart intact. Opening the gates years ago to Zafira had only brought him heartache. It had been a harsh lesson and one that had cemented the resolve to never be caught in the same trap again. Andrei might be his son, and deep in his heart he believed it was true, but until Bogdan saw proof of that, even he would be kept at a distance.

"You disappearing on us in the first place was uncalled for, Bogdan." Arian walked toward him. Based on the gasps of surprise echoing through the hangar, Bogdan and everyone else were shocked to witness Arian locking his arms around the big man. For long moments, Arian didn't say a word. His voice was filled with emotion when he eventually talked.

"I fucking missed you, old timer. Don't you ever do that to us again. You can go wherever you want for however long you need, but you don't just cut off all communication. I need to know that you're safe. Do you hear me, *Tată* Bogdan?"

"Fuck, Arian!" Bogdan's body solidified. It was the one thing he had always envied Viktor from the day of his return and stood witness to the woman he loved holding her son... a son he had wanted to be his. For Arian to honor him by calling him father showed just how strong that bond had been from that first day he had taken his little baby hand in greeting.

"He's right. You've been much more than an advisor to us, and even though you've always been a best friend, you also became a father to us. If not for your guidance over the years since Dad passed away, we would never have been able to thrive in the family business as we did." Vadim gestured toward Vanya who approached them with Andrei's hand protectively around her waist. "Besides, even Andrei admitted that you're the only one who can keep our little sis in line."

"*Destul*, Vadim," Vanya said with a sweet smile.

Zafira

From the look on her brother's face, Bogdan could see he was struggling to come to terms with the change in her. Gone was the spitting cobra who would curse and lash out at the smallest provocation. Pregnancy had softened the hard shell of the Bratva princess. His heart warmed as she hugged his arm against her.

"Besides, our little boy needs his grandfather by his side." She looked at Andrei, who nodded after a questioning look at Bogdan. He was caught by surprise since he had believed everyone would already know about the new development. Vanya continued, thereby confirming they had kept the news a secret until this very moment. "His real grandfather." She all but shimmied on the spot. "Meet Bogdan Rusu, the true and confirmed blood father of Andrei Balan, now Rusu, and the grandfather of our children." Her eyes glowed with excitement and an emotion that swelled his heart to bursting... pride. "And now truly also my *tată*."

"So, Janos Smirnoff was lying all along just to hurt our mother. *Blyad'!* Such an asshole," Vadim said.

"Remember, I did my own investigation after he tried to convince me Viktor was my father," Andrei interjected. "It turns out they did four DNA comparison tests. Only one showed a match to mine. Unfortunately, at the time, the samples were tagged with numbers, and no one could supply names." He shrugged. "I followed my gut and had DNA tests done using a hairbrush of Bogdan's after Janos was killed. The results were conclusive. Bogdan is the man who gave me life."

"So, you didn't only lie to me about Viktor... you betrayed me that night as well, for a second time?"

The blood in Bogdan's body chilled at the clipped words floating toward him from behind. It took all the strength he could muster to turn and face the woman who still seemed to have the ability to crush his soul.

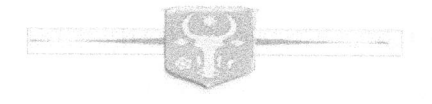

Zafira struggled to keep the anger from exploding inside her as Andrei's words kept milling around her mind, mocking her with the reminder that Bogdan's supposed love had been nothing but a game all those years ago.

"Bogdan is the man who gave me life."

Her father had been right. Bogdan Rusu had been nothing but an opportunist, leeching on the power and wealth of the Guzuns. She had been a fool to keep him by her side as her protector all these years, hoping that one day he would man up and take her away from Viktor... from a man she had come to love and hate with equal fervor.

He had manned up, alright... but only to swing his dick around and fathered a man she had accepted into her life as one of her own.

How fucked up is that? I took Andrei into my heart as if he was my own son. I love that boy as much as I do my own children. And now...

With difficulty, she suppressed the desire to claw at her throat as it felt like she was being suffocated. Betrayal was a hard pill to swallow. This time, it turned sideways in her throat.

"Excuse me?"

Bogdan was suddenly in front of her without her noticing him moving. For such a big man, he had an amazing ability to move as fast as lightning. It took all her willpower to keep her feet cemented to the spot. She refused to cower in the face of his growing anger and resentment.

"*I* betrayed you? Please explain how exactly I did anything of the kind that night, *Ms. Guzun?*"

It didn't slip Zafira's mind that he deliberately denounced her status as *Comare* of the family by using her name—something he had never done before. The tear in her heart slowly stretched wider.

"I was a single man, unattached, if it's even necessary for me to remind you of that fact. I had no reason to keep my dick zipped up... not that night or any other night, for that matter." He leaned closer and sneered into her face. "You made that choice, Zafira Guzun. *You* and you alone."

"Me? *Blyad'*, Bogdan Rusu! You were the one who disappeared. I refused to get married, even on the day of the wedding. I opposed my father until..." She swallowed the words back, suddenly unwilling to blurt out in front of her children, who adored this man, just how corrupt he had been. Her chin tilted back as she looked at him with regal dismissiveness. "And he was right. You never pitched up at the wedding." Her lips curled derisively. "In fact, you didn't show your face until a year later… Do I need to remind you of *that*?"

Bogdan's eyes narrowed ominously as he leaned back to stare at her. "You don't know, do you?"

"Know what?"

"I fucking don't believe this. All these years, I thought you knew… that Viktor would've… he never told you, did he?"

"Told me what? Stop talking in riddles, Bogdan, and spit out what you're blabbering about."

"I was in prison, Zafira. It happened when we arrived back in Moldova, a couple of days after the bachelor party. I was on my way back home from meeting you. I was accosted, knocked out, and I woke up in a hellhole prison in Moscow."

"I don't… but why? How is it possible?" Zafira struggled to keep her composure. "There was no report of this. Why were you even taken into custody?"

"Wake up, Zafira. You've been in this fucking business long enough to know how it works. I wasn't taken into custody. They were paid to make me disappear. I was thrown in that shithole with no court case, no charges. All to make me suffer for daring to fall in love... and I fucking did. I had to fight every day of my life for food and water. To stay alive. It took me a year, but I finally managed to get out of there."

"Why didn't you contact Viktor? He would've helped you."

Bogdan's dark gaze pierced all the way into her soul. She was left feeling vulnerable and raw at the hatred she saw flickering there.

"Viktor? Why would he, Ms. Guzun? When he, his father... and your father were the ones who put me there?"

"My father? Oh my God. It's not enough that you blacken Viktor's name, now you have to attack my father?" Her eyes turned glacial. "While you were the one who latched onto the Guzuns and me for one reason only... money! Tell me, Bogdan, wasn't the ten million U.S. dollars my father paid you to walk away enough? Did you come back and demand more? Maybe from Viktor?"

"Ah... so that's how they turned you against me." He shook his head as sadness filled his eyes. "All these years, I lived in hope, but now I know for sure. You never loved me, Zafira, because if you did, you would never have believed I would have accepted any amount of money to walk away from you."

"But I saw the cleared check! My mother saw it."

"Make up your mind. Ms. Guzun. Did you see it with your own eyes, or did your mother tell you she saw it." Bogdan refused to back down.

"She wouldn't have lied to me. Besides, you didn't have two pennies to rub together at the time. Not that it bothered me since I had more than enough of my own, but—"

"*Comare,* I suggest you think very carefully," Andrei interjected. "It seems you know even less of who and what Bogdan Rusu really is and was from before you married Viktor Guzun."

Zafira glanced briefly at her son-in-law. "What do you mean?"

"It doesn't matter," Bogdan said with a tone of finality she had heard so often over the years. He was done discussing the matter, and no one would change his mind. "If your mother-in-law really wanted information about me, she had more than enough time to use the myriad of resources at her disposal to find it." His eyes glimmered ominously. "That she never did speaks volumes. I now finally accept it, Zafira. It's over. In fact, I doubt we ever truly began."

The words hurt more than if he had slapped her across the face. She might have chased him away, but she had lived in hope every single day that he would return. Walk through her door and take his place as her protector, silently and firmly keeping her safe and cared for without saying a word—like he had done so many times over the years. She had always felt his love when he was close, no matter what had happened between them.

Now, for the first time... there was nothing.

"You are such a fool, *Comare*," Andrei said.

"I don't want to hear it, Andrei," she said in a cold voice.

"You're going to anyway," he said unperturbed. "Do yourself a favor, *Comare*, and use one of those resources Bogdan mentioned, and you will realize just what a fool you have been all these years." His lips thinned. "And just how many lies you were fed about my father... a man who had given up his entire fortune and a life of untold luxury to be trampled on like a cockroach by your father and husband."

"What are you talking about, Andrei?" Arian asked with a warning frown. It didn't matter that they loved Andrei like a brother and Bogdan like a father. They were still very loyal to the memory of Viktor Guzun.

"My father, Bogdan Rusu, was the sole heir of the Grand Duke Matvey Mikhailovich Romanov—had been since he was twenty-one years old. He is the only surviving Grand Duke Romanov. His castle has been serviced and staffed all these years while he continued to be nothing other than your mother's fucking lackey!"

"Mom!" Vanya's scream was the last Zafira heard as pure exhaustion and anemia lost the battle she had been fighting for the past year. The claws of darkness wrapped around her and squeezed, harder and harder until she couldn't breathe.

She didn't realize the strong arms that caught her before she fell were those of Bogdan, who had noticed her losing consciousness and rushed back toward her.

Bogdan... her trusted bodyguard... her protector... and the man her heart just couldn't let go.

Zafira

Chapter Six

A week later, Medpark International Hospital, Chisinau, Moldova...

"*Destul*! I've had enough of this hospital bed. You're all treating me as if I am a frail old woman who had a heart attack." Zafira resolutely pushed off the covers and swung her legs over the side.

"No, you didn't have a heart attack, but you are frail. Don't give me that look. You're malnourished, *Mamă*, which will lead to a heart attack, diabetes, or who knows what!" Vanya's attempt to physically push her mother back into the bed was futile as Zafira slapped her hands away.

"*Blyad'*, Vanya! I'm a grown woman and your mother. You are not going to tell me what to do. I am going home. Now. Today, and no one is going to stop me." She pointed at the hulk of a man who leaned negligently against the door, watching them with amusement. "You brought muscle man for naught. Not even he is going to keep me in bed."

"Well, now that sounds like a challenge, and one I'm more than happy to oblige." His voice sounded calm and filled with ridicule, forcing her furious gaze to slap onto his Goliath frame. "That is if Vanya is willing to leave. I wouldn't want you to embarrass my daughter-in-law by begging me to get under the sheets with—"

"One more word from you, Bogdan Rusu... just one and I'll... I'll..."

Vanya stared at her mom wide-eyed. It was the first time the monarch of the family was at a loss for words. Not only that but her cheeks were also blistered with a rosy glow. Blushing! Zafira Guzun had never done either of those.

"Yeah? You'll what? Chase me away again? Good luck with that." He crossed his arms. "Or did you forget, Ms. Guzun? I don't work for you. In fact, I am *nothing* to you." A tender smile crossed his face as he glanced at Vanya. "Well, apart from sharing a daughter with you and future grandchildren." His eyes turned dark. "Them I will protect with every fiber in my being... even against you, if it ever came to that."

"You *svoloch*! How dare you insinuate that I would ever hurt my own daughter or her—"

"Okay, that's quite enough," Vanya interjected quickly. "If you two want to wash your dirty laundry, I suggest you do so in private before your torrid affair is slathered across every tabloid in the country."

"Rusu is the last man on earth with whom I'd have a torrid affair!"

"I have no interest in an affair with this heartless woman, torrid or otherwise."

The two responses bombarded Vanya from both sides simultaneously. She hid a delighted smile. Her instincts about them had been spot on. Her mother had been slowly withering away ever since Bogdan had left. The haunting look she had seen in his eyes was proof that he also hadn't been happy in Tampa. It was time they set the record straight. One way or the other, they had to find each other.

Vanya wasn't going to rest until she found a way to light the fire between them that had been simmering for as far back as she could remember.

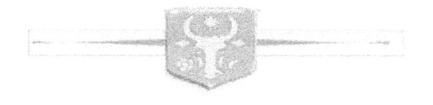

The parking lot, Medpark International Hospital, Chisinau, Moldova...

A shadow in the fading twilight, the man moved with the practiced grace of a cat. His silhouette blended into the surrounding darkness, allowing him to move unnoticed on the rooftop of the building across the street from the hospital. He was dressed in black, his clothing blending perfectly with the shadows.

"Ahh, there you are," he all but cooed as his sharp gaze caught the movement just inside the swivel door. "So, my sources were accurate. Zafira Guzun is in hospital. How quaint and appropriate. Now they can just take you straight to the morgue while your soul joins your useless husband in hell." The words echoed through the air from thinly pressed lips. "*Odio, cazzo* the Guzuns! So, fucking much!"

Settling onto his stomach, he placed the butt of the rifle against his shoulder, adjusting the stock for comfort. His gloved hands gripped the firearm with steady precision as his finger curled lightly on the trigger. Forcing his breathing to slow, he prepared to take aim.

Luciano Maranzano's gaze was sharp through narrowed eyes as he scanned the target area using the rifle's scope. His mind was calm and focused, a stark contrast to the tense anticipation that seemed to hum in the air. He adjusted the scope slightly, aligning the crosshairs with his chosen target. Usually, he would have appointed an assassin for the task, but after what the Guzuns and Andrei Balan, who now apparently changed his name to Rusu, had done to him, he didn't trust anyone. More than that, he wanted the satisfaction of being the one to snuff out their last breaths... one after the other. Starting with the Matriarch of the family.

He waited, allowing the world to fall still around him. The distant sounds of the city faded, leaving only the soft whisper of the midday breeze. Time seemed to stretch as he prepared to take the shot. The weight of the moment hung in the air. The door swiveled open, and as he had seen many times before, the Goliath, Bogdan Rusu, hovered over Zafira, protecting her from harm with his humongous body.

With a final, controlled breath, Luciano gazed through the scope.

"No... they have to suffer first. Fuck what *he* wants. I'm not doing Zafira first. She must go last. That's what I want. For every single Guzun to suffer the loss I had to with my grandfather and father at their hands. And once they are broken and vulnerable, it'll be their turn." His face hardened. "Not to mention what that fucking Andrei did to me." He cringed at the memory of the furious man cutting off his manhood. Shaking off the depression that threatened to pull him under, he peered at his target one more time. "No, they have to suffer." Decision made, his finger relaxed from the trigger as he moved the scope to gaze at Vanya who followed behind her mother.

"Now, what do we have here?" A delighted laugh exploded from his lips. "The bitch is breeding! Oh, now, isn't that just perfect? Andrei Rusu, it's going to be such a pleasure to make you suffer." A cruel seed took root in his mind. "You're not only going to mourn the loss of your lovely wife, Rusu. You're going to regret the day you ever met me." He remained still for a moment, watching the three people climb into a black GMC SUV. Only once the convoy of four cars moved out of sight did he rise and dismantle his rifle.

"Finally, I have found a way to make Andrei Rusu pay for what he did to me. And believe me, you bastard, you'll suffer for as long as you breathe air."

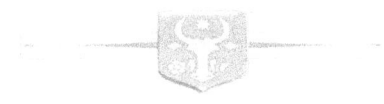

A luxury yacht in the Black Sea, one-hundred-and-fifty miles off the Romanian coast...

"What do you mean you decided she has to die last?" The anger in the man's voice wasn't suppressed well. In fact, he made no effort to hide the irritation from Luciano Maranzano. He was beginning to realize more and more that he had made a mistake in trusting the Sicilian mobster to take orders. As a once god-like Don of the Mafia, he didn't abide well to conforming to the wishes of others. The fact that he had orchestrated and prepared his own escape from imprisonment should've been warning enough.

Even though he didn't have full access to the cash he had stashed across the globe, he had enough power and support to still garner a force majeure event—the one thing that no one wanted at this point, at least not until they had achieved their goal. Zafira Guzun was situating herself in a position to ride the wave of success on the foundation of what the Maranzanos had been building for years—global power. It was little wonder that Luciano was so furious and willing to do anything to stop her and her family from attaining what was rightfully his birthright.

Zafira

A sly smile turned the man's lips askew. Well, in truth, the Maranzanos couldn't lay such a claim... the birthright could be claimed by anyone with criminal intent. In the end, the accolade would go to the one who rose above the rest. Who had the foresight, the money, and the will to succeed.

Like he did, and no one was going to stand in his way. Not Zafira Guzun and sure as hell not Luciano Maranzano. If the Sicilian refused to follow his orders, he would be the first to walk with the fish, wearing concrete boots. He might have been an ally over the years, but loyalty would only survive if he conformed and realized he didn't have the power he did in the past. A shift had happened while Luciano had been wallowing in self-pity in Estonia.

There was a bigger, crueler, and much more dangerous shark swimming in the waters now.

"You heard me. I have a much better plan in store for the Guzuns." Maranzano resolutely cut him short before he could voice the words rising to his lips. "Don't worry, my friend, what I intend will not only cripple the Guzuns as a whole, but it will also leave Zafira Guzun in ashes. By the time she and her family recover from the shock and horror of what I am going to do, we will already be fully cemented in the position as leaders of global crime."

"If you're naive to believe that I will sit back and allow you to make decisions, you don't know me that well, Luciano. I have too much riding on this to watch Zafira Guzun walk away scot-free. Either you do what I told you to do, or I will find someone who will. You've been playing a cat-and-mouse game with them for years. I sat back watching, but my patience has run out. The time has come to take control. You can walk the path of success with me, or you can happily hop and skip after the Guzuns until your heart's content, but Zafira Guzun won't be one of them. I want her out of the way, Luciano. That is not negotiable, nor is it your decision to decide when she dies."

"You're the naive one if you believe the Guzun Bratva will come to an end should she and her three children die. They have the strongest and most loyal following. Nothing will change. Someone else will step up and continue. Either we cripple them as is my intent so that the entire organization crumbles and comes tumbling down around them, or you can go ahead. Kill Zafira and her brood. Proof will be in the pudding, my friend. You will see that I am right." Luciano cracked a laugh. "My guess is that you already know that. You're too clever not to have done your homework. Me being the assassin isn't going to change the outcome. Now… are we going to do it my way, or are you happy to fail before you begin?"

"What is your way exactly, Luciano?"

"A flash of brilliance, my friend," he preened as he briefly explained the devious plan that had been growing proportionally since the seed had taken root.

"You're right," the man's voice darkened as glee flowed through him. Maranzano had indeed come up with a master plan. He dragged lazily on the cigar, enjoying the calming effect as the nicotine filled his lungs. His eyes followed the white whiff of smoke circling above him before it dissipated into the night. "Very well, but I want to be involved in every step you take. Finalize the details, Luciano. We'll meet in two weeks to discuss the way forward."

"Where?"

"You know the drill. I'll send you the coordinates. Make sure you're in Budapest two weeks from today, Luciano."

"Why the fuck there?" he snapped irritably. "You know how difficult it is for me to travel across borders. In case you forgot, there's a worldwide manhunt out for me."

"I didn't, but neither did I forget how clever you are with disguises. Pull one out of the bag, Luciano… like Tom Cruise in Mission Impossible. I have faith in you. You can do it."

"Fuck you! This isn't a movie—"

Flinging the stub of the cigar overboard, he summarily ended the call. He had no patience to debate the issue with Maranzano. An order had been given. It was time he realized just who swung the scepter in this saga.

Zafira

Chapter Seven

Senzații de Club, located on a private estate on the border of Rose Valley Park, Chisinau, Moldova...

"Welcome back, Master Slayer."

For the first time, Bogdan cringed at the reminder of the reputation that clung to him like a stigma. In certain circles, that was how he would always be remembered. The *ubiytsa smerti*, the death slayer, who cleaned the path of the Guzuns, especially those who dared hurt or threaten the Matriarch and her brood.

Now that he was about to become a grandfather, he wanted to be free from such a moniker. His grandchild was going to remember him as a caring and amusing *grandpapä*, not a Bratva. The decision had been made. He had walked away from the Bratva a year ago. Nothing and no one was going to make him return to a life of murder and mayhem.

"I heard you were back in the city and wondered when you'd show up here." Alin Sava shook Bogdan's hand. "In honesty, I missed your ugly face, my friend."

"And I yours, Alin." A smile slashed over his face. "Besides, you knew I'd be here since it's the only club I ever play at."

"Yeah, strange that. I often wondered why you never scened at the other clubs, even though you accompanied Viktor on the odd occasion over time."

Bogdan's lips compressed at the reminder. Zafira had lost trust in him because he hadn't told her about Viktor's supposed slip at his bachelor party. Little did she know that her beloved husband had enjoyed scening with other women from very early on in their marriage. It had infuriated Bogdan, but he had done his job as Viktor's advisor and friend by keeping quiet about it. Zafira had chosen who she married; it wasn't his place to disillusion her about his fidelity.

"I find I like my privacy as I grow older, which is why I've chosen to limit indulging in the lifestyle to one location. Besides, why would I go anywhere else since I'm co-owner here?"

Senzații de Club was an exclusive BDSM club that only catered to members over the age of fifty. Alin and Bogdan had identified the need for older people who wanted to be able to freely visit a club without bumping into their own children or, worse, their children's friends. Moldova was still a rather conservative community, specifically in regard to freely practicing kink, notably toward the older generation.

"I noticed quite a few masked members when I arrived. Is it theme night?" Bogdan walked out of the private lounge to stand on the balcony overlooking the double-volume entrance hall, which had a dual purpose of serving as the entertainment room where members mingled, danced, or had a bite to eat between scenes.

Alin leaned on the balustrade, sipping on an aromatic bourbon.

"No, but there are a couple of new members or pre-approved visitors who prefer to keep their identities intact." He shrugged. "Since the reason we opened the club was to offer members a safe and comfortable place to practice their kink, I didn't see the harm in allowing the requests. Should I have consulted with you first?"

"Of course not. I was just curious." Bogdan scanned the room below, briefly homing in on those wearing masks. "How do you control it, though? Apart from regular members who have to register their fingerprints to access the club, how do you know that whoever is behind the mask is the person pre-authorized to enter?"

"As you know, visitors are identified via a pre-approved facial scan. Those wearing masks have to agree to the same process in the privacy of my office prior to admittance. We're not allowing anyone in without following the proper protocol, especially since we guarantee our members' confidentiality. It's imperative to ensure everyone stepping foot inside the club has signed an NDA."

Zafira

"You've got everything covered, as usual," Bogdan said. "I think I'm going to take a peek into the dungeons. Who knows, I might just find a recalcitrant sub who needs an attitude adjustment."

"The regulars will be delighted. You've been missed, my friend. Don't be surprised if you get swamped by requests to scene the moment you descend the stairs."

Bogdan waved off the praise and quickly made his way down the stairs. His journey to the first dungeon was interrupted numerous times by greetings and submissives hugging, kissing, and as Alin had said, begging to scene with him.

"I will consider your request, subbie. For now, I'm on dungeon duty." He smiled at the dark-haired woman to soften the rejection as, for the umpteenth time, he cleverly averted committing to play. He wasn't sure what he was in the mood for tonight or if he was even interested in scening. Not with Zafira running around in his mind ever since he and Vanya had taken her home from the hospital over a week ago.

Arriving in the Devil's Dungeon, he was immediately drawn to where a large crowd was gathered around a scene in progress. It soon became clear why. The submissive was boldly topping from the bottom, and even though she was strapped on a Saint Andrew's Cross, the verbal comments were what caused the twittering and laughter from those watching. Bogdan didn't recognize the Dominant, but it was evident how the entire situation embarrassed him, belittling his ability to control the scene.

"If that's the best you can do, perhaps I should be the one holding that strap and not you. Want to swap places, Sir?"

"*Blyad!* What in the Goddamn blazes is she doing here?" Bogdan's gaze zoomed in on the woman. Since she was wearing a full face mask and a pitch-black wig, he had no way of recognizing her, but once his gaze traveled over her lithe form and long legs, he knew... his senses weren't deceiving him. The throaty voice was unmistakable—the firm body belonged to none other than Zafira Guzun.

Zafira

He was aware that Viktor and Zafira had lived a BDSM lifestyle at home, but she had never accompanied him to clubs. Bogdan doubted she even knew Viktor went on a regular basis. To see her here, at his club, broke all the walls he had built around his heart. Here, he could finally be the one in control. His hand itched to spank her rounded ass, so perfectly angled upward in the position she was in. No one had been able to crack the icy veneer Zafira surrounded her soul with. It was time to melt it completely and free the woman inside, clearly yearning to break out of the chains that society and a life with Viktor Guzun had bound her with. Her obvious disrespect in how she kept nudging the Dom was proof of that.

"She's been choosing the wrong Doms since the first day she set foot inside the club." Bogdan looked at the man standing beside him. He hid his surprise as he recognized Antonio Baritva, although he shouldn't have been since he had handpicked his successor to take over protecting Zafira. Antonio wouldn't allow her to venture out anywhere alone.

"Makes one wonder why she bothers," Bogdan chose not to acknowledge the association Antonio had with the subbie on the Saint Andrew's Cross.

"Perhaps she's been waiting for the right Dom to take over and give her exactly what she needs."

Bogdan didn't respond. Antonio was right. Zafira was a proud woman and would rather be pushed into accepting a scene than agree to one she might not fully comprehend the end result. Hence, choosing Doms she could easily manipulate, hoping he would lose control and whip the hell out of her.

"I didn't figure her as a masochist."

"No? Maybe a Dom with just the right balance of sadism is the kind to establish whether she is one and to what extent." Antonio shrugged. "Or maybe she isn't and just needs a proper whipping to remind her that she's still alive."

"I don't think we're talking about the same woman." Bogdan refused to consider that Zafira might have suffered more than she led on. She was a strong, assertive, and confident woman. One who ruled the Guzun Organization from behind the scenes in such a clever manner, not even her children were aware of the power she exerted within the criminal world. Nothing happened in the EU Bratva world without her knowing. Why would a woman like her succumb to emotions… and if she did, what were they… and why now all of a sudden?

When the crowd burst out laughing after another scathing remark from the masked submissive, Bogdan stepped in.

"I believe that is quite enough." He held out his hand, and the Dom gladly relinquished the strap.

"Thank you, Master Slayer. I'm Dom Sergei. I don't know why she approached me if she's after a sadistic spanking. That's not my scene and I refuse to be ridiculed into complying." He smiled grimly. "Except my tactic to coax the needy submissive to the surface only resulted in teasing the brat in her more."

"No matter, I will take over," he growled softly. Although he had been out of town for over a year, Alin had kept him up to date with club matters. He recalled Sergei's details, a gentle club Dominant who preferred coaxing a sub rather than punishing them. "What is the scene she's after?"

"What the devil is going on? *Blyad*! I didn't come here to—" Zafira's attempt to twist her head to see who her Dom was consulting was stemmed by the position of the cross and by the voice cutting her protest short.

"*Destul*! You will be quiet." Bogdan's Dom voice was dark, guttural, and a thick brogue that made everyone stare at him. He sounded completely different.

"She wanted a spanking and offered sex, but only if I could make her cry." The Dom smiled. "I wasn't looking for sex tonight, but the challenge would've been to break through the ice layer she so proudly carries around."

"Meaning?" Bogdan stared at Zafira. Her body was stiff as she bore back to try to hear their conversation.

"It's in her eyes. Inside, she's as cold as an iced-over lake, but there's more. Deep inside, I detected a desperation for something else... perhaps a need for someone who could reach past all the chains locking the woman inside and allow her to soar to the sky."

"If she wants to cry, why not find a sadist?" Bogdan rammed his hands into his pockets in an attempt to still the tingling in his palms, the itching to do just that… make her cry. As the Dungeon Master on duty, it fell to him to conduct discipline where a submissive blatantly disrespected a Dom she agreed to scene with. It was part of the protocol and club rules everyone had to adhere to. The same would apply to dominants who overstepped the boundaries.

"Apparently, it's an old habit of hers. She has been coming here for the past ten months and always chooses dominants who love brats and allow them to manipulate the scene. This is the second time she approached me. The previous time was just after I joined the club. That night, she came very close to crying."

"So, you thought perhaps this time you would find the trigger like you did then." Bogdan's hands turned into fists. "How often does she come here?"

"Twice a month. Always on the second and the twentieth. For some reason, those two dates must be significant in her life."

Bogdan's heart beat rapidly as adrenaline pumped through his veins. Perhaps he had been wrong about her. Maybe she had gotten better at hiding her emotions. The second of February was the first night they had made love in the year when she married Viktor. The twentieth was the last night they had spent together—the night he had declared his love and urged her not to marry Viktor, promising her that they could build their own future together—was also the night he was thrown in jail.

Or perhaps he had it all wrong... maybe it was because she hated the memory of what they had shared that made her yearn for physical pain and tears.

Well, la dracu. *It's time to find out. If the mighty* Comare *wants to be whipped until she cries, I'll be too happy to oblige.*

Chapter Eight

Crack! Crack!

"Holy *yebat*!" Zafira's cry of shocked surprise and pain at the unexpected strikes on her bottom immediately quieted her loud protest at being ignored.

Instinct warned her it wasn't her chosen Dom whose hand planted the punishment on her ass. The same dark voice from earlier crawled over her skin, causing it to shrivel with a frisson of fear... or was it perhaps expectation?

This was the kind of Dom she avoided because a strong, powerful Dominant like him would see right through the façade and reach inside her soul to rip apart the shackles she had built over time. The need to be freed from being the strong one and the formidable Matriarch that everyone expected her to be all the time drove her to this club every month. She hoped that there might be one Dom who saw past the brat and freed the woman desperate to break free—the one who had disappeared at the same time Bogdan Rusu had walked away from her and left her to marry his best friend. She had managed to survive all the years because he had returned a year later and had been there—her shadow, her comfort... her heart—until he left again.

That was why she came here... to forget about him while she yearned to find the one Dominant who could awaken the woman Zafira Guzun used to be.

Maybe she had just found him.

"If there is one thing I abhor in my club, it's a sub using a Dom for her own entertainment. Dom Sergei is a gentle giant who only wants to bring the submissive he scenes with pleasure and release. You know that, yet you ridicule him for not rising up to the game you're playing. That, my dear sub, is blatant disrespect." The Dom's voice dipping an octave lower sounded ominous but strangely familiar. Another attempt to look over her shoulder was thwarted by another loud crack of his palm across her ass. "Keep still… unless it's your intention to anger me even more."

"My apologies, Master, but I've met the owner of the club, and it's not you," she managed to grind through her teeth as soon as the pain settled in her mind.

"You met one. I am the other," he said grimly. "I recently returned from an overseas trip, and since I'm the Master on dungeon duty, it'll be my pleasure to correct your attitude."

"I agreed to a scene with Master Sergei, not you, Sir." Zafira knew what his answer would be since the club rules and protocols had to be acknowledged and agreed to every time a member booked a visit online.

"Master Slayer to you, subbie. It doesn't matter whether you agreed to a scene with me. As a Master owner and being on dungeon duty, it's my responsibility to handle punishment. You do recall the club's rules and protocols in regard to misconduct toward other members and specifically to Doms during scenes, right?"

"Yes, Master Slayer." Zafira didn't believe she was a masochist, except on an emotional level, no matter what her attitude portrayed when she scened at the club. Yes, she knew she chose the wrong dominants, then kept pushing them.

Zafira Guzun, the *Comare* of the Guzun Bratva, needed an outlet. One nobody would expect since it was something she never did, not even when her husband had passed away. She desperately needed to cry... hard, loud sobs to release the pain and desolation she had been struggling with since Bogdan Rusu had deserted her a year ago. That he had unexpectedly returned, taken her home from the hospital, then continued to ignore her existence hurt more than she ever imagined it would.

It also confirmed what she feared the most... her foolish heart still yearned for the love they had shared for such a brief period so many years ago.

"First, this will have to come off."

"No! It's one of my boundaries," she protested as he unzipped the dress and ripped off the panties she wore under the leather and lace dress.

Zafira

"A boundary I am surprised no Dom has bothered to push. Be it as it may, it's more important for me to see your skin while I whip you. Even though this will be a punishment, I won't be happy if I cut or bruise your skin in the process because it's covered by a piece of black satin."

Zafira had already realized this was a Master she wouldn't be able to manipulate. She had heard the whispers about Master Slayer and how the masochists missed his presence at the club.

Slayer? Zafira's body turned to stone. Bogdan was known as the slayer of the Guzun Bratva. What were the odds that there were two men in Moldova with the same moniker?

This one is a Dom, Zafira. Have you forgotten what Bogdan thought of you submitting to Viktor?

The question from her inner mind silenced her concern. There was no way this Master was Bogdan. He had never shown any interest in the lifestyle. In fact, he had seemed disgusted with how Viktor had dominated her while at home. More than that, he would never punish her, not even in a scenario such as this. He was too used to following orders. Bogdan would never tell her what to do.

"What the fuck is that?" Zafira's head jerked at the sound of metal balls connecting when Master Slayer swung what looked to be a chain ball flogger just within her peripheral vision.

"From your reaction, I assume you haven't been introduced to a chain ball flogger before?"

"No, and by the sound of it, I don't believe I want to, either."

"Hmm, unfortunately, it's not up to you." A thrill of excitement spread over Zafira's body as the warmth of his breath caressed her cheeks. She could feel his hard body brushing against her back. "Did you or did you not insult a Dom from this establishment in full view of its members?"

The warning in his voice was unmistakable. Her punishment was about to begin. The natural submissive knew she deserved what was about to happen. She nodded with sagging shoulders.

"You acknowledge that you are aware of club protocol and that your action requires punishment as decreed by us?" This time, there was no denying the anger in his voice. Evidently, Master Slayer hated bratty subs who topped from the bottom.

Clank! Clank! Clank!

The sound of the metal balls was ominous, causing her to flinch when he snapped the flogger in the air.

Oh, blyad'! This is going to hurt like fuck. A shudder started at the base of her spine and traveled all the way to her nape. The whipping Dom Sergei had given her would be child's play to what she was about to receive.

"Yes, Master Slayer, I am," she said miserably, knowing if she wanted to be allowed to return to the club, she had no other option but to accept this punishment.

"Even though this is punishment, I expect you to use your safe word if it becomes too much for you. However, I do expect you to endeavor to suffer as much as you can. Is that understood, subbie?"

Zafira nodded again, trembling with fear of the punishment she'd brought upon herself. At the same time, she hoped it would bring her the release she had been searching for… in the form of tears.

"The only time I will accept a nod from a sub in this club is when they're gagged. Are you wearing a ball gag, subbie?"

"No, Master Slayer," Zafira bit out through thin lips. This Dom was becoming very pushy, and her natural brat was hovering very close to jumping off the cliff again.

"Then you will use your voice when spoken to." He pressed his massive chest against her back, proving that he was much taller than her since she was standing on the cross. Her libido stirred to life. "Since you begged so nicely for the kind of scene that will make you cry, it's exactly what I am going to give you. Beware, subbie, this is going to hurt like a motherfucker, so if you want me to stop, no amount of pleading or screaming is going to help. The only word that will end your punishment before I deem it over is the word 'red.' Got it?"

"Yes, Sir."

"Good. Twenty lashes."

Zafira prepared herself when the hard body stepped away and took his heat with him. His warning had been clear, so she expected it to hurt.

Zafira

Mentally, she was prepared, but she had no idea what to expect physically. She had never truly participated in harsh impact tool play. This was going to be more than a lesson. It was going to unhinge her mind.

"Sub," Dom Sergei's soft, cajoling tone drew her gaze to him where he stood by her side. His eyes smoldered with the warmth and understanding that wrapped her soul in benevolence, that assuaged her fears.

"Thank you, Dom Sergei," she said with a tight smile. He was a very nice man and popular with all the submissives. Her disrespect toward him now felt petty and wrong. "I'm sorry," she offered.

"You should be, and even though I feel you're being sincere, I'm afraid your punishment is going to be so much worse than anything you came looking for." His voice lowered. "You wanted to cry, subbie. Prepare to sob your eyes out. Master Slayer has no mercy or time for disrespectful subs."

Zafira barely registered the swish of the flogger when the most excruciating pain seared through her body.

"Aaawww! Fuck!"

Bogdan waited, noticing how her nostrils flared as she attempted to breathe through the pain. Her eyes were tightly squeezed shut.

Clank! Clank!

Another lash impacted hard, causing her to snort air through her nose as a scream of pain exploded from her lips.

"Here we go, subbie. Let me hear you cry." He brought the lashes down in a blur of quick snaps of his wrist.

Her screams sounded blunt and filled with horror as they echoed through the dungeon. With every strike from the metal flogger, her body slammed back against the cross, her whimpers pitiful.

Bogdan's lips flattened as he witnessed the signs of pain chiseled into her tormented face. As a sadist, he enjoyed giving and experiencing the joy of the pain that harsh punishment offered, but he always limited his actions to the experience of the masochists or subs.

When it came to impact tools, he preferred to use them in an erotic, sadistic scene. At least that way, he could push the sub harder and farther, offering her an out-of-body experience through the addition of controlled pain. With Zafira, he acknowledged that he was acting out of anger. Not because of her unruly action toward Dom Sergei but in remembrance of her chasing him away when all he wanted was to declare his love. With a sigh that signaled discord for his own unacceptable behavior, he reduced the impact of the strikes.

Zafira was close to giving in to the threatening black void that hovered at the edge of her consciousness. It was there in the tautness of her shoulders, the way her face contorted—he had witnessed the signs more than enough to identify her wavering control. That wasn't what he wanted.

Zafira Guzun needed to cry, and the sadist in him wanted to watch the tears roll over her cheeks.

"*Isus Hristos!*" she screamed as the metal balls struck painfully inside the velvety folds of her labia. The first lone tear rolled over her cheek.

"Ah, beautiful," Bogdan praised as he aimed the next strike at the swollen nub of her clitoris.

"*Blyad!*" The curse burst forth in a garbled shriek as tears now coursed unchecked down her cheeks. Deep sobs shuddered through her body, followed by a low wail that slammed against the walls. "Red!"

Bogdan stopped flogging her immediately, then smiled when her body trembled and twisted as the sudden loss of pain triggered an orgasm to race through her. Her breathing was harsh as she struggled to catch her breath while sobs still tore through her.

"Easy, subbie," he purred in her ear as his hand on the small of her back gentled her shivering body and calmed her down.

"No! I need... this is too much... *sob*... I need... please, Master Slayer. I need..."

Zafira

Bogdan's body turned to stone. He knew what was coming. Since this was punishment, he shouldn't accommodate her, but he did anyway.

"You need what, subbie?"

"Fuck me, Master Slayer. Please fuck me!"

"I sincerely doubt that swollen and tender pussy of yours could handle the pounding I'd give you, subbie, so—"

"Just fuck me! Now, Master Slayer."

Bogdan could've just done as she demanded, but the beast in his soul prodded him to torture her a little more. To see just how far gone she was. How desperate she was to find the full release her body and mind craved. He circled her and caught her chin in his hand, forcing her eyes to him. The disbelief in Zafira's eyes flashed for long moments as her breathing turned choppy and shallow with shock.

"So, subbie... now that you know exactly who I am, do you still want me to fuck you?" Bogdan prepared himself for another tongue lashing... to once again be chased away with his tail between his legs.

"Yes, Master Slayer," she surprised him by saying in a clear, confident voice. "Fuck me now!"

He was behind her without remembering he had moved. Without preamble or preparing her for his huge ten-inch cock, he slid his turgid length balls deep inside her.

Her scream echoed throughout the dungeon, causing a flash of pleasure to race through Bogdan. His jaw turned rigid as she climaxed upon entry. Her muscles gripped him so hard, he winced. It was as if she had been created just for him, fitting him like a custom-made glove.

"Still breathing, subbie?" he said with his voice soaked in amusement.

"Who needs air," she wailed. "Just fuck me."

Bogdan drew his cock back, plowed into her again, and lost it as she shattered once again. This time, he didn't stop but powered into her, his hips driving like a jackhammer. Slow was not an option; he didn't even try. He didn't care whether she was ready for more as he started the deep and brutal rhythm. He fucked her so hard, so deep, he slammed her into the wooden cross with every thrust into her.

"Holy fuck!" Bogdan was blinded by lust, by the need to find quick release. He lost control over the rush of need as explosions of pleasure ripped through him, obliterating the world around him.

"*Blyad!* Yes," he grunted as his release ejaculated inside her with such force that his knees buckled. His fingers dug painfully into her hips, and still in a daze, he knew that she would be bruised from the tight grip. It didn't matter, not when a high, desperate wail escaped her lips as she came once again, this time so hard that every muscle of her cunt tightened and pulsed around him.

Bogdan desperately dragged air into his lungs, forcing his body to calm down. He was overwhelmed by the sense of belonging that rushed through him. More so, the feeling of ownership that ripped every ounce of despair from his soul. Nothing could bring him down from feeling ten feet tall.

Zafira Guzun had just made a huge mistake. She was his now.

His voice sounded strained but was as dark as the devil churning inside him when he said against her ear, "You belong to me now, Zafira. Remember that. Offer what is mine to another, and he's a dead man."

Zafira

Chapter Nine

Four days later, at a private airstrip near Kramář's Villa, Prague, Czech Republic...

"What the *blyad'* is he doing here, Antonio?" Zafira stopped in her tracks as she identified the huge man standing by the black convoy of SUVs waiting for their arrival.

"Fuck if I know, *Comare*." Antonio's voice was stern, but a quick glance his way confirmed the undertone of amusement she detected in his tone.

"Fucked is what you'll be if I find out you told him of this trip," she sneered through thin lips as she continued walking. "You, more than anyone, know how delicate this situation is."

"I didn't say a word to anyone, *Comare*, but since he's been a part of this situation from inception, you know as well as I do that if there's anyone who would know exactly how delicate this scenario is, it's him. Perhaps he overheard you discussing using the Guzun's private plane for this flight with Arian?" Antonio said in a hushed tone as Bogdan Rusu politely opened the door for Zafira, who blatantly ignored him and got into the vehicle with her usual feminine grace.

"I wouldn't put it past him to listen in on another's private conversation," she snapped as Bogdan closed the door and walked around the SUV. His usual stoic expression didn't convey him having heard what she said. What did surprise her was that Antonio got into the driver's seat, and the uninvited asshole settled into the seat next to her. "I prefer to have the seat to myself."

"Tough shit, I'm not moving." He ignored her indignant gasp at his rude comeback. His gaze remained fixed ahead. "You need added protection since you stubbornly refuse to consider your own safety by coming here after what happened at that restaurant in Bílovec a week ago."

"If I need anything, Rusu, you can rest assured you'd be the last person on earth I'd ask."

"Good thing you didn't have to ask then, isn't it?"

The words were growled in a low tone... one that reminded her of his Dom voice at the club. Her pussy was still sensitive, reminding her every time she sat down that he had shown her no mercy when he had whipped her. Brutally and systematically breaking down every emotional defense she had raised against him over time.

Her cheeks exploded with color as she recalled how wild she had been. A veritable nymphomaniac who, once having a taste of the dangerous nectar he offered, couldn't get enough. Even now, angry and indignant that he boldly invaded the secure little world she had created for herself, a seam of unbridled lust opened inside her, setting her loins aflame. She shifted uncomfortably.

"I thought you were going to Russia with Vanya and Andrei. Aren't you supposedly the DIY king my daughter believes is going to convert the nursery into a little paradise for my grandson?"

"Our grandson."

"There seems to be many contentions on that matter. How sure are you that Andrei is your son?"

Zafira did her best not to flinch at the deadeye he cast her way.

"I have always trusted Andrei, and he has no reason to lie to me. He sure as hell has nothing to gain."

"Not even a coveted title of Grand Duke Romanov?"

"I can't decide whether you've become delusional in your old age or only played the role of a fearless *Comare* all these years or if this heartless, mistrusting, cynical woman is who you have always been, and I was just too smitten to realize it." He didn't bother looking at her. "Andrei is the most honest man I have ever met. You know it as well as I do. Besides, with what he inherited from Janos, he doesn't need anything from me... least of all a stupid, useless title."

"If you have such a low opinion of me, why are you here?" Zafira had to muster all her inner strength to keep her voice from trembling. In the position she was in, many insults had been flung her way over the years. From this man, they were like an arrow piercing her heart. "Surely, you don't give a shit whether I live or die?"

His head swung her way in slow motion. The look in his eyes was one she hadn't seen before, maybe because in the past, as her protector, he had kept it all hidden from her—reproach, disappointment, and most of all, regret.

"If you said those words to me a year ago, I would've said, you're right, I don't. Now, after finding you at *Senzații de Club*, I believe I'd like to keep you alive a little longer. I've got some seriously kink fucking I still want to do with you."

"*Du-te dracu*, Bogdan Rusu. Do you hear me? Go to hell! If you think I'll become your sex slave just because... just because..."

"Just because you begged me to fuck you over and over," he offered helpfully.

"Fuck off, Rusu. The only reason why that night happened was because I was already vulnerable by the time you arrived. I sure as hell have no interest in becoming your fuck buddy."

"Oh, I don't need a fuck buddy, Ms. Guzun. There are many queuing already for that position. What I want is to free the true woman you've kept buried under all those layers of coldness and indifference for years. Now that I have tapped into her, I am going to unleash the full force of her need." His eyes darkened. She quivered as his Dom voice rose from the depths of his being. "No one is going to feed off her desires but me, Zafira. Make no mistake about that. You are mine now, and I don't share. Best you remember that. As I warned you that night, any man who touches you..." His eyes glowed ominously. "Will die."

"We have arrived, *Comare*." Antonio's gruff announcement cut short any response Zafira was about to offer—not that she had one ready since his words and the dark warning in his eyes caught her off guard. This was a different Bogdan Rusu. The protector he had been the majority of her adult life was no more. In his place was a devilish beast, stamping his ownership... protecting his prey... his mate.

Zafira

Zafira didn't know whether she should be elated or shit scared. Truthfully, she was a little of both.

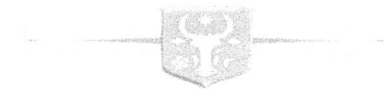

The home of the Czech Republic's Prime Minister, Kramář's Villa, Prague...

Marek Cermak welcomed Zafira with obvious happiness and exhilaration.

"Bogdan? I'm surprised to see you here," Marek said as he shook his hand. He glanced at Zafira. "Or did I misunderstand the last time we spoke? I was under the impression he's not with the Guzuns anymore?"

"Seems your impression was incorrect, Prime Minister Cermak," Bogdan growled over the explanation Zafira started to voice. "I am here to ensure Ms. Guzun's safety, especially after the horrendous way your armed forces broke up a birthday party she was attending in your city not so long ago."

The hefty man's cheeks turned a shade darker under Bogdan's direct stare. "Yes, that was a rather unfortunate incident. Too much force was used, but I assure you, I've already put corrective measures in place."

"Too much force? What about the innocent women and children who were killed in the shooting, Prime Minister? A shooting that was in no way justified since no guest present at the restaurant carried any weapons."

"As I said, the matter is being dealt with."

"Strange that there was even a raid at a private restaurant housing an intimate function that posed no danger to anyone, isn't it?"

"Enough, Bogdan. You are souring my visit with my friends," Zafira interjected when she noticed Marek shifting uncomfortably. "Besides, Marek's doing all that needs to be done to correct the matter."

"Ah, so I imagine everyone who was arrested has been released," Bogdan said with a wide smile. "Imagine what it would do to you running for the presidency if it came to light that people were incarcerated on the back of an illegal raid." Bogdan demonstrated a downhill slide. "Just like that, your dreams go down the drain."

Bogdan shrugged off Zafira's frown that threatened castration with a blunt knife.

"No need to give me that look, Ms. Guzun. I only speak the truth."

"Is that true?" Zafira looked at Marek. "Has everyone been released? I remember reading that Artem Melnyk was also arrested that night on suspicion of being involved with the Solntvesoka Bratva. I've known the man for years and never once suspected him of being capable of the cruel acts he's being accused of."

"I wish it was that easy. Unfortunately, since the law has found just cause to interrogate him, Artem Melnyk won't be released until a full investigation has been completed." Marek lit a cigar and dragged the smoke deep into his lungs. "Ultimately, we need to look out for the safety of our people. If Artem Melnyk is who Interpol believes him to be, it's for the best he remains under lock and key."

"Oh, I couldn't agree more," Zafira looked around. "Where's Triska? I hope we didn't arrive at an inconvenient time. I have a business meeting tomorrow, so I thought to pop in and say hi first."

"You know you're always welcome, Zafira. Besides, our friends' anniversary is coming up." Marek smiled broadly. "Remember? Vanya and Azja's birthdays are next month. Thirty-four years. Good Lord, suddenly I feel so old!"

"I can't believe it's been that long. It's rare to find friendships that last. At first, I had thought we'd be like ships sailing past at sea, but over time, we've just grown closer." Zafira laughed as Triska walked into Marek's study. "There you are. I would've been devastated if you weren't here."

"I would've been, too. It's been so long since we last had a good visit. Tell me you're staying over. Yes! You'll be sleeping in the guest wing and have dinner with us tonight."

Bogdan didn't miss the sharp warning glance from Marek, nor did it slip his attention that Triska ignored him and continued to woo Zafira into staying.

"C'mon, Zaffie! Please stay."

"Actually, I am only here for the day," Zafira began tentatively.

"I don't see why not, Ms. Guzun," Bogdan said, keeping his gaze locked on Marek. "Your meeting is tomorrow, and you have nothing pressing for today, so we can stay one night."

"I'd appreciate it if you don't make decisions on my behalf, Bogdan," Zafira sneered under her breath. "You have no insight into my calendar, and I—"

"Don't I?" He kept his response clipped but soft so their interlude couldn't be overheard.

Zafira bore back as she glowered at him. One eyebrow crawled higher as, once again, the beast inside him purred with satisfaction at her reaction. The Matriarch was clearly not happy that he knew so much about her movements.

She was about to be even less happy with him.

"Ms. Guzun will stay for the night but only if I am invited to overnight here as well." He shrugged. "Can't let her out of my sight, I'm afraid."

"Bogdan Rusu!" Zafira stamped her foot in annoyance.

A grin flashed over his face as he glanced down at her. She looked like a little girl playing grown up with her foot tapping on the floor, hands on her hips, and her brows pulled into a straight line. The flash in her eyes caught his mirth, and she licked her lips, a sure sign that she had forgotten what she was about to say. Then her chin tilted back, and she blasted him with a look all the way from Iceland.

"If anyone stays to look over me, it'll be Antonio. He works for me. You don't."

"That is true, but since I gave Antonio the rest of the day off, you're stuck with me."

"You gave him the day off? Since when..." Zafira exhaled slowly as she realized how animatedly the two Cermaks were watching their interlude. "We will deal with this later, make no mistake about that, Rusu." She spun away and smiled at their hosts. "Of course, I'll stay. Bogdan doesn't mind sleeping in the car."

"He sure as hell minds," Bogdan growled.

"I will never allow a guest to sleep in his car," Triska protested at the same time.

"Well, thank you, Mrs. Cermak. Your hospitality is appreciated." Bogdan offered her a toothy grin.

Zafira made no secret of her annoyance as she glared at him. He shrugged it off. Something was up with the two Cermaks. Zafira came here to find out what kind of danger Artem Melnyk held in store for her and whether he had let anything slip about the Novaya Volna Group and the Shadow Don while under interrogation. The gentle probing over dinner didn't achieve any success. Marek was as closed-lipped as a zipped plastic bag.

Bogdan's inner beast scratching at his insides every time he looked at Marek Cermak warned him that he wasn't who he portrayed to be. For some reason, Bogdan had never trusted this man as much as Viktor and Zafira had. He never ignored that warning sign. It was the sixth sense that had guided him his entire life, kept him alive and alert.

This time, the intensity of danger he felt thrilling inside him was like the mortality rate of a black mamba's snake bite—the kind of odds he wasn't prepared to take with Zafira's life.

Zafira

Chapter Ten

Midnight, Kramář's Villa…

Bogdan didn't say anything when he was allocated a room on the other side of the Villa from where Zafira would sleep. It did, however, confirm that his suspicions about the Cermaks were right. There was something they were withholding from Zafira.

Checking his watch for the umpteenth time, he paced the room. He hadn't been sitting around idly waiting for Zafira and Triska to finish giggling over the olden days. Instead, he had excused himself early to contact Vanya to do some dark web background checks on the couple.

"Watch your back, *Comare.* Triska might be a dear old friend, but they are the ones whose betrayal can cut the deepest," he grumbled as he kept an eye on the patio where the two women were still happily drinking wine and reminiscing. Well, Triska might be having fun and getting drunk, but he knew Zafira well enough to know she would be fishing in-between with fine-tuned expertise for information Artem Melnyk might have divulged during interrogation.

Interpol was known for using brutal techniques if they believed they had just cause. Since the Pakhan of the Solntvesoka Bratva was classified as one of the most dangerous criminals in the world, anyone thought to have an association with him would be put through the wringer. Artem Melnyk was a strong man, and Bogdan didn't believe he would give in to torture.

"Except everyone has a price," he muttered as he leaned against the door. If the agent in charge had done his or her homework on the kind of life Artem lived, all it would take to make him spill the beans on other Bratva leaders would be a coffer full of cash and full exoneration from being prosecuted in the future.

Zafira

"The cherry on top would be that they could very well go that far," Bogdan mused out loud.

Like with many of the Bratva families, leaders kept their identities hidden from the outside world. The Guzuns were a prime example of how successfully they could live a double life. No one, apart from the selected few, knew what the Pakhan of the Solntvesoka Bratva looked like or what his real name was.

"In searching for accolades that they finally made leeway in catching one of the most dangerous mobsters in the world, the stupid assholes might just hand the very man carte blanche without even realizing they had him right under their noses."

The buzz of the cell phone drew his attention from his pondering. With eyes steadfast on the two women, he answered on the second ring.

"What did you find?" he said without preamble.

"If I wasn't so pissed off at what I'm looking at, I'd give you a proper head scrubbing for answering the phone in such a rude manner, *Tată.*"

"Vanya, now isn't the time for niceties. If your mother is in danger, I—"

"You're right, but do remember in the future," she said sweetly before dragging in a deep breath. "It's not pretty, and Mom is going to be devastated when she finds out how they've been deceiving her all these years. Well, her and my father... actually, all of us. Worse... the people of the Republic of—"

"Enough with the senseless chatter! Start talking, Vanya." Bogdan might have walked away from Zafira a year ago, but that didn't mean he cared any less for her, her family, or her safety... especially after the night they had spent together at *Senzații de Club*... but for now, those emotions were securely locked away for further unraveling later. Keeping her alive was now his only priority.

"I'm afraid there are some dark forces underfoot in the Cermak household, *Tată*. I suggest you get my mother out of there immediately. From what I uncovered, I believe they're not to be trusted. My gut instinct tells me Mom's life is in danger."

"Why? Spit it out, *printsessa*. I need to know what I'm up against."

Zafira

Bogdan's jaw locked as Vanya began talking. His hands curled into fists as he considered how to break the news to Zafira. Though normally slow to anger, betrayal from trusted friends was the one thing guaranteed to ignite his temper. He pictured her reaction—those usually inexpressive eyes widening in disbelief, her lips parting as if to protest before pressing together in denial until, eventually, she would feel the sting of this betrayal as deeply as he did.

Yet convincing her to leave tonight would not be easy, especially since he was the one who had argued so passionately earlier to stay. Of course, that was before he had the information he was now armed with.

"Fucking idiot! I should've done due diligence the moment I found out she intended to come here," he growled through his teeth, anger simmering, but took a deep breath to calm himself. Losing his temper would not help convince Zafira to amend her beliefs about the situation. He had to approach this carefully, appealing to her reason and making her see why they had to leave immediately.

A brief glance out of the window confirmed that the two women had finished their wine sessions since the patio was deserted.

With a grim expression, he checked his weapons, grabbed his backpack, and with determined strides, walked toward the opposite wing where Zafira would be getting ready for bed. Since he had done reconnaissance before retreating to his room, he knew which hallways to avoid where guards were posted. The intent was to leave the premises unseen, without anyone the wiser, including the Cermaks, that they had gone.

"Our room is just around the corner. If you need anything, just holler."

"*Blyad'*," Bogdan cursed as he pressed his body as flat as he could against the wall as Triska's voice floated toward him. Luckily, she turned in the opposite direction of the hallway from where he attempted to melt into the wall. Releasing the breath he was holding, he didn't waste any more time, and within moments, he slipped quietly into Zafira's room.

Zafira

"What the actual fuck!?" Her voice rose with anger, but she didn't attempt to cover her naked torso as she spun around to notice him inside her room. "I suggest you get the hell out of here, Rusu, before I kick your ball sack all the way up your ass until you choke on it."

"Stop the melodrama, *Comare*. However enticing your naked body might be, sex isn't why I'm here. Get dressed. We're getting out of here. *Grăbiți-vă*, Zafira. I want to be in the air out of Chez airspace before Cermak realizes we're gone."

"I am not going anywhere. At least not—"

The soft buzz of Bogdan's phone cut her protest short as he held up his hand and answered the call.

"Yes, Antonio?" He listened intently. "Good. Make sure the plane is warmed up and ready for take-off the moment we arrive." Bogdan wasn't idle during the conversation. He quickly stuffed Zafira's clothes in her carry-on and flung a pair of pants and a sweater on the bed. "Get dressed, except if you want your tits flapping in the air while we run."

"My tits do not flap, I'll have you know," she snapped but surprisingly started getting dressed. A glacial look chilled him on the spot. "For now, since I can sense the urgency in your manner, I will concede and do as you say, but do not think this is the end of it, Rusu. The moment we're in the car, you better start explaining your actions."

"Of course." He headed toward the door. "Oh, for fuck's sake," he growled as he looked over his shoulder to find her in front of the mirror. "Leave your hair. No one is going to see you, and I assure you I don't give a shit whether your perfect coiffure is in place or messy and sexy."

"As if I give *a shit* either way," she flung back but was on his heels when he opened the door.

Bogdan knew he was being a prick and that his attitude toward her had changed since his return, but that had come along with the shift in their relationship. She was no longer the mighty *Comare* whose heels he clipped wherever she went or stuck to her side like a leech because the love he felt for her demanded closeness.

No, he had dissociated himself from that role and was done being an *extra* in her life. It was time she realized he was no longer one of the family's soldiers who danced to her tune and admired her for her spunk. He was a man with enough power and money to build his own empire, should he choose to. A Dominant who knew exactly what he wanted. She had already given herself to him… she belonged to him, whether she believed it or not.

"Hmm," he murmured loud enough for her to hear. "The lady doth protest too much, me thinks."

"*Poshel na khuy*, Bogdan Rusu."

"Fuck you? With pleasure, Ms. Guzun, but it'll have to wait until we're in the air. I have no intention of rushing it, so a quickie in the back of the GMC with Antonio watching us in the rearview—"

"You're on thin ice, Rusu. I'm not some brainless twit, and I refuse to be ridiculed. Once we're back home, I want you to disappear from my life. If I never see you again, it'll be too soon."

"Such contradictory words and actions, Ms. Guzun."

"Shut the fuck up, you *svo lach'*, and get us out of here, or did you forget your supposed urgency to leave?"

"I didn't forget, but at least your constant denial of your attraction and lust for me was entertaining during our escape."

"I am not attracted to you, and I'm sure as hell not lusting after you." Zafira climbed into the back seat and glowered at him. "You have become demented, Rusu. Probably because your brain has shriveled with age." She snorted. "As will your dick if you dare swing it in my direction on the plane."

"*Ah, malen'kaya Comare*, that's the kind of challenge the Dom in me just can't resist. Very well, now we're definitely fucking on the plane."

Zafira slammed the door in his face as he moved to get in next to her. His deep chuckle reverberated through the air as he quickly jogged around and got in.

"Yep," he stretched out and closed his eyes, settling in for a short power nap as Antonio pulled off. "We're going to fuck all the way back to Moldova."

Chapter Eleven

Twenty-one-thousand feet in the air... thirty miles past the Czech Republic border...

As the private jet soared through the night sky, Zafira found herself lost in thought, her gaze fixed on the vast darkness outside the window. The city lights below twinkled like distant stars, a stark contrast to the luxury within the cabin.

The interior of Arian's Bombardier Challenger 600 was nothing short of opulent. Plush leather seats beckoned with their promise of comfort, accented by polished wood and gleaming metal fixtures. Soft ambient lighting bathed the space in a warm glow, casting shadows that danced gracefully across the cabin walls. Everything exuded an air of refined elegance, a testament to her son's impeccable taste and lifestyle.

Yet, amid the lavish surroundings, Zafira's mind was consumed by a tumultuous mix of emotions. She couldn't shake the feeling of discord that had settled within her since their abrupt departure from Marek Cermak's house. Bogdan's insistence on leaving had left her bewildered and frustrated. She trusted him implicitly, but she couldn't help but question his judgment in this instance. Marek had been a friend for years, a confidant she had relied on countless times. She refused to believe that he or his associates posed any danger to her.

Glancing over at Bogdan, Zafira felt her heart skip a beat despite her inner turmoil. He was a formidable figure, even in his mid-sixties, with a presence that commanded respect. His silver hair was neatly trimmed, framing a ruggedly handsome face weathered by years of experience. Beneath the warmth in his piercing gaze glimmered a hint of steel as a reminder of the strength that lay within him.

Zafira

Broad shoulders and well-defined muscles spoke of a lifetime of discipline and dedication.

"Well, Rusu?" Zafira finally spoke, breaking the tense silence that hung between them. "I'm waiting. Just why the hell did we have to leave Marek's so urgently?" Her tone was rigid from frustration and curiosity.

"All in good time," Bogdan rumbled as he released his safety belt, got up, and did the same with hers. "For now, it's time to honor the promise I made in the car."

"Let me go!" Zafira bore back as he pulled her from her seat. "You can stuff your promise so far up your ass that you choke on it. I have no interest in having sex with you."

"No? Hmm… like the delightful petrichor of early morning rain, the aroma of your lust teasing my nostrils says otherwise, so stop pretending, Ms. Guzun. Be honest about your needs for once in your life."

"My needs? What do you know about my needs, Rusu? You've been by my side for over forty years. In all that time, twenty of which I was a widow without a man by my side, you didn't address my so-called needs or cared whether I attended to them. Not once! So, what the fuck gives you the right or makes you an expert on my needs all of a sudden?"

Bogdan didn't bother to respond. Instead, he picked her up, draped her over one shoulder like a bag of potatoes, and carried her toward the private bedroom at the back of the plane.

"*Poshel na khuy*, Rusu. *Pyeryestan'!* Put me down!"

"Yep, that's what we're gonna be doing, but I'll be the one fucking since you don't seem to be interested."

"I'm warning you, Rusu. I'm going to rip you a new asshole if you don't let me go."

"Such eloquence," he mocked as he shouldered his way through the narrow doorway without lowering her. Once inside, he dropped her unceremoniously on the bed, smiling as she bounced, her legs and arms all over the place.

At first, Zafira didn't move, too angry to react, until his gaze traveled over her body.

"Pervert!" she said contemptuously. Even though she was wearing pants, her widespread legs appeared too inviting. Scrambling back, she sat up, folding her legs under her.

"Still in denial, Zafira? Even after our night at the club?"

His smooth, gravelly voice tore open an opulent seam of flourishing sexual desire that cocooned the nerve endings in her loins. Her breath caught as shards of heat spiked through her core.

The tip of her rose-colored tongue brushed her lips as she stared at him. Unbeknownst to her, the desire for him was evident in her eyes. Regardless, the usually confident *Comare* was suddenly unsure how to act, what to say, and petrified he would change his mind and leave her high and dry in her lustful state.

"Well?" he prodded.

Zafira knew he wouldn't give her a quarter. This wasn't the Bogdan Rusu who followed orders. This was Master Slayer, the Dom who had full and complete control over her as a submissive. He had come into his own as a powerful and confident man who knew what he wanted, and although he could easily take her without asking, he wanted her to admit she needed him. In her heart, she had already given in to him. As the mighty Matriarch, she refused to back down too quickly.

Bogdan might be the more experienced seducer between the two of them, but he was no less affected. Her eyes smoldered as she detected pearlescent beads of sweat situated in a random design on his upper lip.

Closing her eyes, she slowed her breathing to calm her nerves and arrest the unabating throb in her loins in anticipation of an almost certain outcome about to unfold. It was useless to refute what Bogdan already knew. She wanted him, and she was done denying herself the pleasure only he could bring.

"Well? What is it you want from me, Bogdan? Acknowledgment that your dominance excites me? That I have never climaxed as hard or as many times as I did with you that night at the club? That even now, in denial, my loins are on fire and my clit is throbbing incessantly? That I need you to control my body, do what you did that night, and unleash the woman inside me? Yes, Master Slayer... I admit to all the above and more." She slowly pulled off her sweater and leaned back on the bed, her naked breasts glowing in the soft downlights of the cabin. "So, what more do you want to hear, Bogdan."

"That'll be quite enough for now," he said in his dark Dom voice that sent a fresh wave of heat rushing into her loins.

She was enthralled by the sudden roughness in his voice and the expectant look on his face. His arousal was apparent in every flex of his thickly muscled frame.

"You're slightly overdressed for what I have in mind. Lose the pants and shoes, subbie."

Zafira briefly pressed her thighs together, suddenly desperate to curb her sexual excitement. The instantaneous chemical attraction and reckless impulsiveness for him were a foreign concept to her. It scared her but excited the hell out of her just as much. Watching him undress to his tight Calvin Klein boxers, she quickly shimmied out of the pants and kicked off her sneakers.

"Lie back and spread your legs wide open."

"Bogdan, I don't— *Blyad*! What was that for?" Zafira wailed as she rubbed the burning palm print on her upper thigh.

"You've been in the lifestyle long enough to know the dynamics have changed, subbie."

"Sweet fucking hell," she mumbled. "You could've just told me... *Master Slayer*," she emphasized the moniker in a clipped voice.

"I shouldn't have to, my pet." His voice turned a shade darker. "Now, do I need to repeat the instruction?"

"No, Sir." Still, she hesitated. In the light of day, she wasn't as confident as she had been that night in the dungeon or later in the private room, high on endorphins. At sixty-four, her skin wasn't as tight as twenty years ago, and she didn't have the perfect pink labia like the younger subs. Suddenly, she felt old, flabby, and wrinkled.

"Now, that kind of attitude is only gonna piss me off. You are beautiful, Zafira. In my eyes, you have always been the perfect woman... you still are."

Zafira

Zafira shouldn't be surprised that he read her insecurities so accurately. He had proved himself to be one of the most powerful dominants she had ever come across.

"Thank you, Master Slayer," she murmured as she reverently spread her legs wide open.

"That's better… and very, very pretty indeed." For long moments, he just stared. The heat sparking in the depth of his eyes set her mind at ease. He wasn't lying. He found her attractive, beautiful even, and he lusted after her… as much as she did him.

"Hmm, since I didn't plan for this, I don't have my toy bag with me, so we'll have to improvise."

"Improvise what? We don't need any toys, Master Slayer. You've got hands, fingers, and a very large tool to play with. Fucking only requires two things. A hole and a pole… so what are you waiting for?"

Zafira smiled impishly as Bogdan burst out laughing. He laughed from deep within his soul, as if he had finally lost all darkness inside him. It was the most beautiful sound ever.

"That's what I love about you, subbie. You can make me laugh." His continued chuckle chased after him as he opened the door and unconcerned with his state of undress, headed toward the galley at the front of the plane. Zafira scrambled up and quickly slammed the door shut. He might parade his big dick covered in only a tight pair of boxers, but she'd be damned if anyone would see her spread open like a ripe fig!

Chapter Twelve

"Ready to play, subbie?" Bogdan said as he returned soon after. He smirked as he gestured at her legs. "Hook your arms through your legs and pull your knees up to your ears. I want that ass of yours lifted high."

"Ehm... it doesn't sound like a very comfortable position, Master Slayer."

"Do as you're told, subbie. I have no compunction about punishing you before offering pleasure. It's up to you how we continue."

"I thought a scene was supposed to be a mutual agreement," she mumbled as she gingerly pulled herself into the instructed position.

"You gave me your agreement to give your body what it needs the night at the club, Zafira.

Remember? Unconditional submission was the terminology we agreed upon."

"For that night, yes!"

"Oh, no, I told you in the dungeon that you're mine now, and that means unconditionally mine."

"What the hell is that?" Zafira's eyes homed in on the root he held in his hand.

"Come now. You love cooking. Don't pretend you don't know what this is." The amused grin was back on his face as he sat down beside her. Spreading her ass cheeks wide, he spread some olive oil on her rosette.

"Master Slayer, ginger is in no way or form appropriate for what you're doing." Her attempt to jerk away was fruitless as he prodded the tiny hole.

"I'm sure you've heard of the terminology figging before," he said colloquially.

"*Blyad*! There is no way you are shoving that up my ass!"

"No? Then I suppose we'll agree to disagree," he said with a wide grin.

Zafira glared at him. He was having too much fun at her expense.

"You have no need to worry about discomfort. See?" Bogdan held up the ginger root. It was narrow on one side with a slightly wider base where he had tied a white string. "Almost like a butt plug."

"I hate butt plugs," she protested as he carefully pushed it into her asshole.

"There," he said as he checked to ensure it was deep enough with the string hanging out for ease of removal later. "I assume you have never been figged before."

"I sure as hell haven't."

"Ah, then it's a cherry-popping moment, so to speak."

"If you mention another kind of fruit or vegetable, I'm going to kick you in the head, Master Slayer," Zafira threatened as she loosened her hold on her legs.

"No, keep them there. I want full access to every part of your body as well as seeing your expression."

"I'm still waiting for the fun part... my fun part since this seems to be all aimed at your pleasure, not mine," she muttered incoherently.

"Patience, subbie." Brushing his hands down her tight flanks, he leaned forward and placed a lingering kiss right on her clit. Her loins flushed her pussy with liquid heat, which, in turn, set her clit throbbing wildly. "The ginger root will warm your rectum, so you experience a subtle burning sensation. However, I suggest that you don't clench your ass muscles."

"Why not?"

"The burning becomes hot. Very, very hot. That's the downside, but the upside is that it increases stimulation, resulting in hard and continuous climaxes."

"Oh fuck," Zafira whimpered as the first wave of warmth from her ass penetrated her mind.

"Normally, when I play with ginger root, I deny the sub climaxes, but in your case, I'm going for the opposite. So, subbie, you can come as often and as hard as you need to."

"I hate forced climaxes, Bogdan," she snapped acerbically.

Crack! Crack!

"Holy shit," she screamed as her ass cheeks clenched from the painful strikes. Heat exploded inside her ass.

"Call me Bogdan once more and I'll use my belt. Is that clear?"

"Yes, Master Slayer." Zafira's breath was choppy. He had just pushed the damn root up her ass, and it already burned like Satan's breath.

"I've been hungry for this little nub," Bogdan growled as he buried his head between her thighs and locked his lips around her clit.

"Oh, *blyad*!" Zafira moaned and thrashed against his face as he alternated sucking and nibbling until her mind was ready to combust. At the same time, the scorching hot sensations he had warned her about were triggered. Lust sped through her veins, leaving her helpless against every wave of eroticism that he unleashed, intensified by the heat in her ass.

An orgasm rushed through her with such suddenness, her breathing became haggard as she thrashed against the hold she had on her legs. His warning to keep them there flashed through her mind, and she clung to them as her entire body clenched through the ripples that threatened to unhinge her.

"Beautiful, but try not to lose your plug in the process, subbie," Bogdan praised as he shoved the ginger root that was being pushed out back inside her ass.

Zafira forced breath into her lungs, doing her best to keep her anus from clenching and unclenching in tandem with her throbbing clit.

Crack! Crack! Crack!

"*Isus Hristos!*" Zafira screamed as his large hand planted three brutal slaps right over her pussy and clit. Her hips lifted, and her ass clenched. "Nooo," she cried as it felt like her ass was invaded by a flood of lava.

After six orgasms, the intense burning subsided somewhat. The heat was still intense, but it was more of a warming feeling, a sort of minty-tingly buzz that kept her aware and on the verge of the need to come.

Still, the devil Master wasn't satisfied as once again his palm cracked across her buttocks. Over and over. Her screams echoed through the cabin as she writhed against the unpleasant combination of pain, heat, and lust.

"No more. Fuck, please. Have mercy," she pleaded as his fingers plucked at her clit before pushing two fingers inside her. With precision, he tapped them against her G-spot. "Shit," she gasped in surprise as a climax rolled over her.

"I want your eyes on me, Zafira. Open them and keep them on me."

Reluctantly, she opened her eyes. She had kept them closed in an effort not to allow him to see her vulnerability. He hadn't been fooled. Lifting her head, her lust-filled eyes seared him. It soothed Zafira's tortured mind to notice the way his cock strained against his boxers. He was rock-hard and suffering as much as she was.

"That was the last one, subbie. You don't come again until I fuck you. Is that clear?"

"You've got to be kidding me!" Zafira knew there was no way she'd be able to hold back, especially since there was no warning with the intensity of the effect the root had on her. No tingling, no tightening of her clit... just a rush when the climax already ripped through her.

"Do not disappoint me, subbie."

His deep voice resonated inside her, awakening the subconscious desire to please him... her Dom, her Master Slayer.

"I won't, Master Slayer," she vowed softly as she resolutely tightened the hold on her legs.

For the next ten minutes, Bogdan pushed her to the edge, over and over, until she was writhing in desperation, thrashing, pleading, cursing, and then pleading again.

"That was beautiful, Zafira. You did so well, my subbie. I'm proud of you," Bogdan said as he slowly removed the torture-root from her ass.

"There, relax, my pet," he cooed as he forced her hands to release her legs, and he carefully assisted her in straightening them. Her moans were a mixture of bliss and pain when he gently massaged the muscles in her legs until she was completely relaxed.

"So... are we ever going to get to the fucking part?" Zafira demanded once she was breathing normally. It didn't matter that she had come so many times that even her teeth hurt. Her pussy wanted more... it wanted him—his hard cock taking possession of her, pounding her into Kingdom come.

Standing beside the bed, Bogdan dropped his boxers. Zafira drooled as his rock-hard cock jutted out in a perpendicular arch. Precum glistened on the velvety tip. She swallowed hard, watching as he stroked his cock with slow, measured slides. Her nipples were hard little buttons, painful in her need.

Tired of waiting, she got on her knees and ran her hands up the inside of his legs.

"I love how big you are, Bogdan." This time, he didn't reprimand her, but his breath hissed through his teeth when she feathered her fingers over his nipples.

"Fuck, subbie," he grunted as she licked his balls before locking her lips over one and gently sucking it into her mouth.

"Hmm... I've been wanting to do this for over forty years," she whispered as she licked along the length of his cock with the flat of her tongue. Opening her mouth, she wrapped her lips around the base of his cock before dragging her mouth toward the tip, sucking greedily en route. "Ah, sustenance from the Master himself," she cooed as she sensually licked off the precum still oozing from its center.

"Enough," Bogdan growled. "I want to pound your cunt, not spill my jizz inside your mouth."

With a delighted giggle, Zafira locked her lips on his tip and sucked him all the way down her throat.

"Now you've done it," Bogdan growled as he pulled his hips back to release his cock from her mouth. Picking her up, he threw her back on the bed, following her down to return the favor, and lapped at her hot, wet pussy.

Within seconds, Zafira was right back where she was not so long ago, shuddering and needy. Kneeling between her legs, he applied his magical mouth and tongue on her clit and inside her pussy, pressing and licking her perineum. As he feasted on her, he inserted two fingers into her ass.

"Still breathing, subbie?"

"If you don't fuck me soon, I might combust, then we both lose," she managed grimly, forcing back the impending climax. Like Bogdan, she wanted to come with him pounding inside her.

Her entire system zinged with the desire to feel his huge cock impale her. To find out if the confusing sensations that coursed through her were going to fling her just as high as they did when he fucked her at the club.

"Pull up your legs again, subbie. I want you to watch."

Zafira didn't question the command and immediately clamped her knees beside her ears.

He continued to toy with her pussy and her clit, pinching her nipples until she panted. She dragged her hips higher and gasped, her eyes locked on his tongue, lapping and licking deep inside her pussy. She had never felt as alive as she did at that moment. Every nerve sizzled like it had been lit by a bolt of electricity dancing across her skin.

"Fuck me. I need you, Bogdan. Please, baby."

Moving onto his knees, he positioned his cock at her entrance. With one hand, he gripped the base and teasingly moved it up and down her labia until she was wet and sticky with need.

"Oh, fuck," she gasped as he finally started pushing his cock inside her, deeper and deeper until he was balls deep. "I have never watched this. It's so... fuck, it's hot!"

"Indeed, my pet, and it's about to get hotter," he promised as he pulled his cock back. It was the most erotic sight she had ever seen—his massive, hard shaft withdrawing from her clenching, needy flesh.

Then he pushed back in, slowly, gently, and with a deep warning grunt, "Hold on, subbie. This is gonna be rough," he started pounding into her.

Bogdan held onto her thighs for balance as he settled into a brutal rhythm. Hard and fast, he filled her deeper than she thought possible, stretching her as he pounded into her. Zafira was mesmerized by the sight of their primal fucking.

"Mine. Just mine." His voice sounded dark and dangerous.

Every rational thought escaped from her mind. The sensations swirling through her possessed and overwhelmed her. She was flung so high, the pain and pleasure merged into a magical euphoria.

Bogdan fucked her forcefully, punishingly, and she loved every second of it. Still, she suspected he was holding back. Her eyes lifted to his.

"I want to fly, Master Slayer. Give me all of you. No more holding back."

"Remember you asked for this, Zafira," he warned as with a primal roar, he slammed back inside, filling and stretching her to the maximum. He was buried so deep, his nut sack squeezed tight at her entrance. He completely impaled her.

"Fuck. That hurts! Fuck, I love it," she shrieked on a broken breath. The powerful undertow finally struck in a confluence of physical and emotional currents that sucked her under. It ripped away her balance and pulled her, gasping up the face of a towering rogue wave—lifting her up, then crushing her beneath its weight.

"Bogdan, stop. I can't! It's... fuck!"

Her plea turned into a scream as her body tightened. Warm liquid gushed from her loins. Her hips jerked as she clawed at her legs in a desperate attempt to draw a breath.

"No stopping, subbie. This is what you asked for. What your body needs." Bogdan relentlessly powered into her, subsuming her in an act of carnal pleasure as he kept fueling her orgasms, triggering one after the other to stagger through her body.

Zafira was helpless against the paroxysms that rocked her. Long waves of ecstasy rolled over her as she fought off the dull ache of excess. She surrendered, splayed open with her legs pulled up, her ass high in the air, as she twitched and jagged in submission to his control.

With the sexually induced alchemy of physical sensations, she became overwhelmed. She knew now that she loved him more than she had realized. No one but him could draw every raw emotion from the depths of her soul and offer her unbound pleasures.

A final wave of ecstasy swept over her, tearing away the last of her control and leaving her shattered in his arms once again.

Zafira

"That's beautiful, my pet," Bogdan grunted, flayed bare and ragged as he came inside her, pumping and convulsing, squeezing her as he wrapped his arms around her waist.

"God, I can't breathe," Zafira gasped as he finally allowed her to lower her legs and massaged them again.

"Breathing is overrated, subbie." His smile was evil. "Better power up. This is only the beginning. We have another good three hours of flight still to go.

"You're kidding, right?" Zafira was too tired to do anything but blink at him in disbelief.

"Nope. I promised to fuck you all the way home, and that's exactly what I intend to do."

Linzi Basset

Zafira

Chapter Thirteen

Ferma La Guzun, the residence of Zafira Guzun, nestled on the banks of the Dniester River, Dubasari, Moldova...

"I'm done waiting. You had better start talking quickly, Rusu. My patience is rapidly running out. Why the hell did we have to run away like scared rabbits in the middle of the night from very good friends of the family?"

"Calm down, Mom," Vanya said soothingly. "Bogdan only did what was the best for you."

"I'm not a child or incapable of defending myself, Vanya. I don't need to be treated like a porcelain doll, for one thing."

"Well, excuse us for wanting to have you around long enough to meet all our kids," Vanya snapped. "You forget that you nearly died not so long ago. Someone is out to kill you, so if you think for one minute we are just going to idly sit by and watch that happen, you don't know us very well."

Zafira's heart sank as she looked into the worried eyes of her children. Their fear and concern for her safety were palpable. The sobering realization jolted her out of the single-minded focus she had maintained for so long. In her relentless pursuit of building a covert group to counter Luciano Maranzano's ambitions and to maintain the kind of Bratva group her father had supported when he had offered Viktor his backing, she had lost sight of the toll her actions were taking on her loved ones.

Vanya's words cut deep, a painful reminder of how close she had come to losing everything. Her children had already suffered the trauma of her nearly dying once before, yet here she was, recklessly pursuing a way to get rid of Maranzano and placing herself in harm's way once again. The weight of her actions pressed heavily upon her. A surge of guilt washed over her.

Eyes softening, her gaze shifted from Arian to Vadim to Vanya and Andrei, taking in their concerned expressions and the unspoken fear that lingered behind their eyes.

Blyad'! I've been so blind to the emotional turmoil I inflicted upon them. In her quest for acknowledgment as a fearless *Comare* and her desire to protect her family, she had inadvertently neglected the very people who meant the world to her.

She blinked back the unexpected tears burning her eyes as realization hit her like a ton of bricks. If she wasn't careful, her family could become collateral damage in her crusade. The thought of losing them was more terrifying than any threat she personally faced.

I'll never let that happen! I'm supposed to be their protector, not them mine!

"You are right, my darling. I have to be more aware, especially of your feelings and needs. I've been selfish, I know, but it's only because I'm trying to keep you all safe."

"It's not your job to keep us safe, Mother," Arian said gruffly. "That's on us. We're adults now, and we were brought up to take care of ourselves. We all made a promise to Dad that we'd protect you. So, it's on us. We're the ones who should take care of you."

"Arian said it," Vadim added. "You've done your job by teaching us the values of life and protecting us as kids. Now, it's our turn."

"I already—"

"It's useless to keep protesting, Mom. It's been said, and so it shall be." Vanya hugged her fiercely. "Besides, you have to be there to help me with my little one. I have no clue about being a mother, and I'm shit scared I'll fuck it up."

"For one thing, you should stop cursing. Parents shouldn't use bad words in front of their little princes." Bogdan shifted his weight but ignored Zafira's sardonic glance. "He'll be catching on quickly enough as it is. We don't want fuck or *blyad'* to be his first word."

"Heaven forbid," Andrei agreed with a smile. "*Tată* would be my preference, of course."

Zafira

"Dream on, big boy. Our son's first word is going to be *Mamă,* and that's it." Vanya walked into Andrei's embrace. Their love shone from deep within, enhanced by the trials and tribulations they had to endure to finally find each other again. The new life growing inside her had only strengthened the golden thread weaving their souls together.

"What the fuck!?" Before anyone could comprehend what Bogdan's furious cry was about, he stepped in front of Zafira, lifted her off her feet, and dove behind the sofa. The Ming vase on a side table exploding into hundreds of pieces alerted everyone of the danger. "Sniper outside. On the outside perimeter fence," Bogdan growled as he got up and confirmed that he hadn't smashed Zafira into the ground with a gruff, "Are you still breathing, Ms. Guzun?"

"Who can breathe when squashed like a bug by your lug of a body," she snapped as she slapped his hand away and got to her feet. Her eyes rounded, and she went pale as she noticed blood on his sleeve. "You've been shot!"

Bogdan glanced at his arm. "It's a scratch. Come, boys," he said as he brushed her hand away before stomping toward the side door. "Let's catch the motherfucker."

"It's a waste of time," Zafira said, concerned about Bogdan's wound. "He's long gone by now."

"No, he's not. I just saw a reflection to the right of where the shot initially came from. He's trying to ascertain if he got the hit."

"The hit?" Zafira pressed herself against the wall. "Get down, Vanya, and stay low." She looked at Bogdan. "Are you saying there's a contract out on me?"

"You didn't know?" He shook his head as he cautiously opened the sliding glass door. "Tsk-tsk-tsk, *Comare*. You're slipping." Glancing over his shoulder at Vanya, he said in a clipped tone, "Protect your mother." Pointing in three directions, he continued, "Vadim, you and Antonio go around the house to the left. Andrei, you, and Arian to the right. I'm going to skirt around and approach the fuckface from behind. I want him herded. If there's a chance of him escaping, shoot to incapacitate, not kill. I want to know who the fuck sent him."

Zafira was in awe of the natural way Bogdan took charge. He had always been the one taking orders and performing them without saying a word. To see him exerting such powerful confidence without effort set her heart racing. This was the Bogdan she had fallen in love with all those years ago. The one who wasn't scared to take charge and shot the stupidity of his friends down when he didn't agree with what they were doing.

Then why did he allow them to force a wedge between us? Why didn't he fight for me when he returned a year later? Was it because he truly never loved me?

The loud boom of a gunshot outside shattered her thoughts.

"No!" With fear rushing through her like a destructive tornado, Zafira raced toward the front door, only to be tackled onto the sofa by her fiery daughter.

"Don't be stupid, Mom. Running outside is going to draw all the attention to you, and it'll only end in disaster... for our boys. They'll forget to take care of their own safety in an effort to protect you." She smiled as she raised her trusted Molotov pistol. "Besides, I've got you."

"Someone was shot, Vanya. I've gotta go look. What if it's—" She bit back the words that threatened to explode unchecked from her lips. Her feelings for Bogdan had always been kept close to her heart. She had never shared it with anyone, not even her gorgeous but obviously very clever daughter.

"Don't worry, *Mamă*. I'm sure Bogdan is fine. Besides, my newly acquired *tată* has too much going for him now to allow any pitiful assassin to end the life of the *ubiytsa smerti*. If anyone is shot, it's most probably the motherfucker who was stupid enough to come to *your* home, believing he'd get away scot-free." She giggled as she peeked over the back of the sofa. "Have you seen how he has changed, *Mamă*? So powerful, demanding, and issuing orders left, right, and center, and not one of our big, bad boys blinked an eye. They just jumped to attention and did his bidding." She slapped a hand on her thigh.

"Now *that's* the Bogdan I knew he was. I'm so stoked he finally found the power and confidence within himself."

"It's always been there, my darling," Zafira said softly as realization struck. "He just kept it suppressed… because of me."

"I have a question, and I'd appreciate an honest answer." Vanya scrutinized her mother's expression. "Why have you kept your feelings from Bogdan all these years? It's been so long since Dad's death, and still, you keep him at a distance. Don't you think it's time to admit that you love him? Or do you really want to grow old alone?"

"That's three questions." Zafira felt her face heating as a blush crept over her cheeks under Vanya's examination.

"Humor me," Vanya said. Her expression was resolute, warning Zafira that she wasn't going to back down.

"I don't believe anyone wants to grow old alone. The prospect of that is quite depressing." Vanya once again foiled her attempt to peek outside by yanking her down behind the sofa.

"Stay out of sight, please. Continue, I'm listening."

"Good Lord, you're bossy," Zafira complained but sagged down next to her, a ragged sigh confirming that she had given up fighting her very determined daughter.

"Who said I'm in love with Bogdan? Just because you and Andrei found each other doesn't mean everyone else should follow suit. Besides," she quickly continued before Vanya could voice the words hovering on her lips. "It's more important to get Arian and Izolda back together. He hasn't said a word about her apart from telling me she left him. Nor has he made any attempt to make contact with her. It's not right. He loves her, and she loves him. They belong together. They always have."

"Hmm, that does sound so fitting... and not only for Arian and Izolda, don't you agree, *Mamă*?"

"Enough, Vanya. You're digging where there is no tree to plant."

"Am I? I may be younger than you, but I'm not stupid. I know you, and I know Bogdan. I've watched the two of you all these years. No matter how hard either of you deny it, you love each other. I'll be fucked if I know why you are both so hardheaded and not owning up to it." She shook her head.

"Time waits for no one, Mom. Once it passes you by, you can never get it back. Don't wake up when it's too late. You're worried Bogdan is the one who got shot. What if it was him, and he's dying or already dead out there?" Vanya's eyes sparked as Zafira turned pale. "Yeah, just imagine losing him without ever telling him how you feel or living with his lovemaking every moment of every day for the rest of your life? Wake up, *Mamă*, or the time will come that you will regret you never did."

It was a vision that shook Zafira's equilibrium. Even while Bogdan had been away, the days had been long and lonely, but she had always known he was there... somewhere, alive and within reach. All she had to do was call. He would've come without question.

Vanya was right. The time had come to put aside her pride. Life was giving her a second chance with Bogdan.

All she had to do was take it.

Linzi Basset

Zafira

Chapter Fourteen

GUZUN
BRATVA

A couple of miles from the farmhouse of Ferma La Guzun...

The underground dungeon was dark and damp, lit only by a few flickering torches along the stone walls. Water dripped down from the ceiling, collecting in small puddles on the cold floor. Chains and shackles hung menacingly from various points along the walls and pillars. In the center of the room, tied securely to a wooden chair, sat the assassin—slender and dressed all in black, with sharp angular features and jet-black hair. Dried blood caked one side of his face from a wound sustained during his capture. Pale gray eyes flashed defiantly as he stared at the three men who had strapped his hands and ankles tightly to the chair.

With expressions hard and unforgiving, Bogdan, Vadim, Arian, and Andrei watched him for long, stretched-out moments.

"Talk, motherfucker. Who hired you to kill the *Comare*?" Bogdan finally demanded in a low but firm voice.

The assassin merely smirked. "I work alone." Regardless of his taunting smile, he jumped slightly when Bogdan slammed his fist down hard on a nearby table.

"*Marcire all 'inferno!* We know someone sent you. You fucking tell me who, or I will beat it out of you."

Refusing to be intimidated, the man sneered with a laugh, "Go ahead and try. You'll get nothing from me."

Arian's fist closed around the assassin's long hair to yank his head back sharply, eliciting a small grunt of pain. With his face mere inches from the assassin, he hissed, "Unless you talk, you're of no use to us alive."

The assassin set his jaw stubbornly. "Then do you fucking worst, but I'll tell you shit."

"Beating him up and pulling his hair isn't going to achieve shit," Bogdan growled as he drew his dagger and pressed it up to the assassin's throat. "Talk fuckface. I want a name." He ignored the man's wincing as the sharp edge sliced through his skin. The blood seeping from the cut quickly soaked his shirt like a blooming carnation.

Still, the assassin laughed mockingly, proving why he had been chosen for the daunting job. The sound was cold and ruthless as it echoed off the dungeon walls. "Do what you will. I'll die before I break my oath."

"He's not going to talk. My patience has run out. Just kill the motherfucker. I'm done wasting my time, especially since we all know who's behind this."

Bogdan was surprised at Arian reaching the end of his tether so quickly. He was the one who could stretch out a questioning for hours on end. This time, he wanted out of the dungeon within thirty minutes.

"Yeah, we know whose tune he's dancing to, Arian, but I want to know where to find that bastard.

I'm not going to do the same tango as we did before with Maranzano. You stopped Andrei that day from killing him. This time, I'll make fucking sure he won't be coming back." His gaze sharpened. "To do that, I need to know where to find that bastard before the next prick he sends has a lucky strike and kills your mother."

"What do you propose, *Tată*?" Andrei asked as Arian and Bogdan retreated from their captive. He slowly circled the bound man, who watched him with growing trepidation. Andrei's questioning techniques were well-known among assassins in the criminal world but would be preferable to the *ubiytsa smerti* taking charge. He flinched visibly as Bogdan picked up two knives and started sharpening them over a whetstone. The grating sound echoed ominously through the dank room.

"For the quickest way to get him to talk, I have a mind to revisit an old Viking torture method." Bogdan's eyes flicked over the assassin's muscled frame. "He's a strong fucker, so he'll last long."

"Is it gonna make him talk before he dies?" Vadim interjected from where he leaned against the door.

"If he doesn't, he'd be a fool."

"There's no torture that'll make me talk, fuckface, so you might as well kill me now. I'm not ratting out anyone." His bravery evaporated as the giant man turned and walked closer.

"Thanks for the offer, but where's the fun in that?" Bogdan pressed the sharp point against his face, cruelly cutting through the skin, leaving his chin to gape open wide. "Nawh, since it's been a while, I aim to have some fun today." He looked at the three men over his shoulder. "Ever heard of the Blood Eagle procedure? It's rather a graphic and disturbing process but very rewarding when the wailing and pleading starts."

"*Isus Hristos*, Bogdan, that's gruesome. I hope you're gonna clean up after you're done," Vadim protested. "There's no way I'm picking up lung tissues and ribs off the floor."

"No need. I'll just send in the dogs to feed on his insides." Bogdan continued to circle the chair.

"Wh-What the fuck is a Blood Eagle procedure?" For the first time, the assassin showed a frisson of fear.

"See, that's the problem I have with these youngsters of today. They have no clue of proper assassination methods other than shooting someone. Tsk-tsk, shame on you for giving our profession such a bad rep, fucktard." Bogdan methodically started cutting his shirt from his body. "Usually, this process is done with your victim lying face down on a table, but since the chair has no back section, I'll just do it this way."

"Fuck! Jesus Christ!" the man screamed as Bogdan sliced a thin cut along his vertebrae.

"Come now, that's merely a marker so that when I make the deep cut, I have the right angle." Bogdan walked around to face him.

"Wh-What are you going to do?"

"What does it matter? You said you're not gonna talk, so I'm not going to bother asking any questions. No... I'm doing this purely to have some fun." He tossed the knife in the air and caught it without looking at its trajectory. "But I'm nothing if not a good sport, so I'll explain the process to you. It's quite an intricate procedure, but since I'm not a surgeon, I can't guarantee it'll be done with any finesse." He smirked as the man squirmed in the chair. "We never asked. Do you have a name, or do you prefer fuckface?"

"I'm called *Moartea Neagra*," he sneered and shifted uncomfortably when the blood seeping from the cut down his back pooled on the chair below him.

"Ah, the Black Death." Bogdan snickered, "I've heard of you. It seems you're the one chasing numbers, aiming to have the most kills recorded."

"Isn't he the one who takes any job, even the low-paying and easy ones, just so he can add to how many kills he has under the belt?" Andrei interjected with a tone of disgust ringing in the prisoner's ears.

"The one and only." Bogdan tapped the two knives together. "So, back to the Blood Eagle. Once I've made the cut along your vertebrae, I'm going to start pulling your lungs and ribs out through the wounds. Can you guess why it's called Blood Eagle yet?"

"Fuck you! You can't do that!"

"Once I'm done, it'll form an outline that looks like an eagle's spread wings." Bogdan continued unperturbed and then barked a laugh at Black Death's expression. "The question is how long you would last or if you do hold on until the very end, how soon after would you die, because believe me, the procedure isn't only agonizing, but I'm going to draw it out as long as I can. Eventually, your body will shut down from a combination of organ damage, shock, and blood loss. Either way... at least one of us will have some fun in the coming hours."

"Well, I, for one, am not going to stand around for that. I know how meticulous you can get with these procedures. Every cut has to be perfect. I'll pop in tomorrow morning. Hopefully, you'll be done by then." Arian's words floated over his shoulder back into the room as he headed toward the exit. "You coming, Vadim?"

"Hell, yes. I'm starving. I'd rather have dinner than watch raw meat bubbling out of the poor man's back." Vadim visually shuddered with disgust as he also left the room.

Zafira

"Well, son? Are you squeamish, too?" Bogdan's gaze remained glued on his victim, who was becoming paler by the minute—and the loss of blood wasn't the reason.

"Hell, no," Andrei said with a broad grin. "I'm actually hoping you'll ask for my help. You know... you do the lungs, and I tackle the ribs?"

"That sounds perfect. Let's do this right. Like they do in the movies of surgeons performing procedures—with some music. Put on your playlist. Let's have some tunes rock this joint."

The dull screams of pain and pleas for mercy were suppressed by the rhythmic drums of rock bands until the early morning hours.

Then... nothing.

Silence descended over Ferma La Guzun.

A luxury yacht in the Black Sea, two-hundred-and-ten miles off the Romanian coast...

"You've met Svetlana, I assume?"

Luciano barely looked at the tall, beautiful redheaded woman who sipped on a glass of wine where she was sunning herself beside the jacuzzi on the deck of the luxurious yacht. Since Andrei had cut off his dick, he had no desire or lust-filled moments after women. In fact, he had no desire for any sexual fulfillment. All he was after was revenge. Least of all did he have time to play the kind of games his benefactor was after.

"I have only met one Svetlana, a cleaner in Estonia." He gestured to the lithe form on the chaise lounge. "And that's not her. Why am I here?"

"Yes, your cleaner in Estonia, aka Svetlana Rebane, my half-sister."

"Your what?" Luciano's head whipped around. His eyes narrowed as they caught and held the clear azure gaze, watching him with amusement.

"Come now, Luciano. Don't tell me you've lost your desire for the thrill of the chase through the use of disguises?"

"I don't have time for games. You sent your half-sister to spy on me? What the fuck is this about? I thought we had an agreement." If there was one thing Luciano hated, it was to have people he made fealty with doubt his commitment or loyalty to the cause. This act was like a sucker punch to the gut. He stabbed a finger in the air.

"This, right here, is the reason why I always prefer to work alone. To be the mastermind and the driver of my own fate. I deviated from it before, and that's why I ended up where I did. I refuse to allow it to happen again."

"Relax, Luciano. Svetlana was there to lend a hand should it become necessary." The man smirked. "It didn't, so the precautionary gesture of assistance was wasted."

"Assistance for what? You might be footing some of the finances until I can gain full access to all my money, but don't forget who is in charge. If you were under the impression that I work for you, you are sadly mistaken."

"I see our association more as a partnership, Luciano. One in which both of us wins, especially since we have the same end goal."

"Do we? Pray tell," Luciano leaned negligently against the boat railing. "What exactly is *our* end goal?"

"To kill Zafira Guzun."

Luciano cackled a deep laugh. "Now see, that's where you're wrong. I don't give a fuck whether the *Comare* lives or dies. She might have swayed a couple of spineless older generation Bratva leaders to sniff at her cunt for some fun, but in the end, when push comes to shove, she has no power. She might believe she does, but believe me, Bratva dons are old school. None of them are going to bow to a female's leadership."

"Then it's a good thing I took matters into my own hands. By now, the bitch is dead."

"What did you do?" Luciano suppressed the rage building inside him with difficulty.

"I told you from the start that I want that slut dead. You agreed. It's not my fault that you decided to play a different game." Lighting a cigar, his conspirator took a deep drag and blew out the smoke, watching the swirls dissipate over the ocean before he continued, "I sent the best assassin to finish her."

Luciano laughed. "Finish her? An assassin? Don't you think I've tried that before? That woman has a guardian angel hovering over her head. She should've been dead three times already, and still, she lives. What makes you think your guy is going to achieve success? Come, think about it. You send one measly asshole into a nest of the best assassins in the criminal world, and you believe he got it done? Tell me, my dear man, have you heard from him? Has he finished her, as you say?"

"Not yet, but I have no doubt he succeeded. Otherwise, I would've already been told." The frown on his face showed his uncertainty, but he refused to acknowledge the possibility that the outcome could be failure.

"Good for you then, but I warn you, if he killed either Vanya or Arian Guzun in the process, you will pay the price for fucking up my revenge."

"So, this is why you're doing this? Stupid revenge?"

"It's a factor that drives the hatred inside me, yes, but it's only a side avenue to the main road. I will achieve what I set out to do my entire life—be the global criminal ruler, and no one is going to stand in my way. Not any of the Guzuns…" His gaze on the man in front of him turned glacial. "Or you."

Luciano looked between the two siblings. His eyes flickered briefly as he attempted to marry the redhead with the old cleaner from Estonia. He had to give it to her; the disguise had been top-notch.

"So, my gripe with the Guzuns is well-known. What's yours? Why is it so important to kill only Zafira Guzun?"

"That woman got everything in life that was meant to be mine, then she had the gall to interfere and forced me to adapt and change the direction I was heading. For that, she started paying her debt with the death of Viktor Guzun. Now that I have the means to rule the way I was meant to, it's finally her turn."

"Hold on. You killed Viktor?" Luciano searched his memory. "It's been said that he was killed by Boris Sidorov."

"Oh, Boris and I went way back. He was a means to an end, but his greed and lust for Arian's bitch got in the way. In the end, it was good riddance since it kept my secret secure."

"What secret?"

"Once you have done what we agreed by ridding the world of every single Guzun, I will tell you, because then, my friend, you and I will have the world in our hands. Together, no one would be able to touch us."

Luciano's expression didn't change. This man might be powerful in his own way, but he held no danger for him. If he believed Luciano had any intention of sharing the top dog position with him, he was sadly mistaken.

For now, it suited his purpose not to say anything.

"So, is there anything worthwhile to drink on this tub?"

"Ah, now you're talking. Come... I have a fifty-year-old single malt I've been saving for a special occasion."

Linzi Basset

Zafira

Chapter Fifteen

GUZUN
BRATVA

Two days later, Ferma La Guzun...

"Goodness gracious," Zafira rolled her eyes in a show of dramatization. "You again. Didn't you just leave last night? How many times do I need to tell you kids that I can take care of myself?" Tapping her foot, she opened the door wider to let her brood inside. She glowered at the tall man walking up behind her. "Not that I need to since Goliath has taken it upon himself to move into my house."

"Count yourself lucky, Ms. Guzun," Bogdan growled. "I haven't moved into your room yet. At least you have some modicum of privacy."

Zafira hated the excited thrill that raced down her spine at his words. Having him in her room, in the same bed every night, would be a dream come true. Except she wasn't about to admit as much to the dratted man. He was suddenly too full of himself. Since he had exerted his dominance over her as a submissive at the club and on the plane, she was helpless against his power when he turned all Dom on her.

Blyad'! My panties will slither down my legs without me taking them off. That was what those dark eyes and deep growl did to her.

"So, what's so important that all of you invade my home just before lunch?" One eyebrow crawled higher. "Or did we have an appointment I forgot about in my *senile* state?"

"Stop playing the martyr, Mom. Everyone is here at my request." Vanya all but rubbed her hands with glee as she looked around the room. Vadim sat in an oversized wingback chair with Sabira perched on the arm. His one hand circled her waist lovingly. Arian had arrived alone since he and Izolda had yet to see each other again since she had left him. He was more hardheaded in his old age than Zafira herself. The Matriarch settled in a deep bucket chair with Bogdan standing behind her, his arms crossed over his huge chest. He truly portrayed a veritable Goliath hovering over his prey.

Vanya took Andrei's hand and sat down on the sofa. Her eyes glimmered with happiness. "I went for a 4D scan this morning."

"Why didn't you tell me? I would've gone with," Andrei protested. One hand came to rest on her swollen belly. "Since the smile threatens to wrap around your face, I know it can't be bad news, but c'mon, love, I'm dying here. What's going on?"

Vanya dug the scan images out of her handbag and handed them to Andrei. "Do you see it?"

Andrei stared at the pictures, at first confused, then his eyes widened.

"*Blyad'*... is that?" He looked at Vanya. "Are you saying... *Isus Hristos*, Vanya. Are we having twins?"

"Yes! See! There and there, two little heartbeats." She pointed to the dots on the photos.

"How did they not notice it before?"

"Oh, the doctor had a long medical explanation, but I was too excited and didn't pay attention."

"I'm confused. Twins are usually hereditary from the mother's side. You don't have twins in your family." Andrei looked at Zafira. "Do you?"

"I actually—"

"She does," Vanya cut her off, too excited to keep quiet. "Mom is one of twins, but her sibling died a few hours after birth. Our great-great-grandmother was also one of twins, so there..." Vanya pointed at her belly. "Twinsies! We're having two for one."

"Good Lord, I sincerely hope that doesn't mean you're going to cry and be sweet twice as much as before," Vadim joked, but joy burst from his eyes at his little sister's exuberance.

"You better hope she doesn't morph into Atilla the Hun after the birth," Arian quipped. "I remember how Mom was after Vanya's birth." He cast a sideways glance at Zafira. "Still is, for that matter. Absolutely nothing left of the crying, sweet pregnant woman."

Zafira

"Are you saying I've become unemotional, Arian, barbarian, even?" Zafira's body was as tight as a snare. Indignantly, she stared him down. Yes, she had acknowledged she had become lost in her quest to destroy Maranzano to keep her family safe, but she had never wanted them to notice her inner withdrawal.

"Not so much when Vanya was younger, but ever since Dad passed away, and more so over the past two years, yes, definitely. I'd have to say, even though you're not involved in the family business, you've become distant. You might not realize it, Mother, but you have created a shield around yourself, a guard against anything emotional." Arian was the only one who had the courage to always speak to the heart of the matter.

"Listen who's talking," Zafira snapped. "I don't see your wife by your side, my son. Fix your own fuck ups before you dip your spoon into my porridge, if you don't mind," she snapped but immediately became contrite. "I'm sorry, Arian. I shouldn't have said that. I'm just a little uptight, is all." She got up and with difficulty offered her daughter and son-in-law a bright smile. "I am so happy for you. Come, my darling, we need to start discussing the nursery. I was thinking about the bright, sunny room in the north wing?"

"You want to turn your private den into a nursery?"

"Well, I assume you'll be visiting often once you move to Russia permanently. My grandbabies must have a beautiful room they will love here as well."

"Aww, *Mamă*! That's so sweet."

"And there we go again," Vadim chuckled as the two women walked off, Zafira gently soothing her weeping daughter.

Arian waited until the two women disappeared at the top of the stairs before turning to Bogdan. "You have yet to tell us what you found out from *Moartea Neagra*."

"Yeah, I've been waiting for you to ask," Bogdan said as he sat down. "Here's the kicker. It wasn't Luciano Maranzano who put out the hit on your mother."

"If not him, who the fuck was it?"

Zafira

"You already know what Vanya found, Arian. Why don't you take a guess?" Bogdan ran a hand through his hair. "Before you ask, no, we have no idea what his association with Maranzano is or if they're even in cahoots. Our team is searching the dark web to see if they can find any communication or connection between them, but so far, nothing."

"I fucking don't understand. I thought they had been house friends since Vanya's birth." Arian started pacing.

"So did I, but one thing I can guarantee you is that Triska and Marek Cermak are no friends of your mother." Bogdan leaned forward. "My gut tells me that had I not removed your mother from Kramář's Villa that night, she'd be in her grave by now."

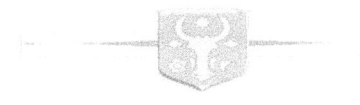

Two hours later, Farma de Pasari, Arian's livestock farm, on the banks of the Dniester River, Dubasari, Moldova...

"How do we keep my mother safe, Bogdan?" Arian asked where he stood, puffing on a cigar in front of the open sliding glass doors leading out onto the patio.

Bogdan didn't immediately respond, studying him for long moments. His sharp eyes picked up on the deep lines beside his mouth and the dark circles under his eyes.

"Are you sleeping, Arian? You look like death woken up."

"I'll sleep when this fucking nightmare is over. I need to keep my family safe, Bogdan. It's my responsibility, and I feel like I'm failing."

"You're not, my boy. You are the foundation and pillar of the family—always have been, even when Viktor was still alive, especially during those last five years of his life. If not for you, the Guzun Bratva would have fallen apart from the direction he wanted to take us in."

"You're right. Dad changed. I never knew why. He suddenly interfered in every decision I made, threatening to take over the reins again. I always believed it was because I was failing as the Pakhan of the group, that he was disappointed in me."

Bogdan's eyes flickered as a heaviness settled in his heart. He hated keeping things from Arian, but his loyalty had always been with Zafira. What Arian didn't know was that Viktor had gotten wind of what she was doing, of the underground group she had started forming in rebellion against how he was squandering her father's money and legacy. Interfering in how Arian had ruled was a desperate attempt at maintaining power that he had lost… not just as the Pakhan of the business but as the husband to a very fiery and confident wife.

"Thanks for that. Perhaps I'm just more tired than I realized." Arian sighed heavily.

"I imagine the situation with Izolda doesn't make your life any easier?" Bogdan dared to prod where no one else would.

"It's over, Bogdan. Trust is such a fickle commodity in a marriage, and it's the one thing we never had." He shook his head. "I shouldn't have married her, especially since I did it for the wrong reasons."

"Because you didn't trust her and believed if you married her, you'd be able to keep a close eye on her? Catch her red-handed when she betrayed you?"

Arian frowned but didn't respond.

"So, how exactly did that turn out for you? Did you catch her betraying you?"

"No. In the end, she truly didn't know that Maranzano was the one pulling the strings. That he had been the puppet master all along."

"Exactly. All Izolda did was play along in an effort to keep you and your family safe... or so she believed."

Arian shrugged. "I let her go, Bogdan, because in the end, she's safer on her own. Being with me comes with the promise of getting hurt or death."

"Yeah, keep telling yourself that," Bogdan growled but didn't pursue the matter as Arian's expression turned dogmatic. "One thing I didn't mention earlier. We did find a connection Merak Cermak had."

"Don't fucking tell me Izolda and—"

"Enough, Arian! For fuck's sake, she's your wife! No matter what you try to make yourself believe, you love her, so stop always making her out to be the bad one." Bogdan exhaled slowly to calm his anger. "The connection I'm referring to is between Marek Cermak and Boros Sidorov."

"Boris? What the fuck would the First Vice President of the Chez Republic have to do with that useless bastard?"

"You forgot who killed Viktor, Arian."

Arian turned pale. "Boris Sidorov. Are you saying Cermak was behind our father's death as well?"

"It's the only thing that makes sense. First, Viktor got killed by Boris, who had a known association with Cermak. He then forced the woman you loved to marry him, and now there's a hit out on your mother—and the assassin that almost cashed out on it confirmed he was the one who's behind it."

"Why would a man in his position take the chance of anyone knowing he's corrupt? Surely, he wouldn't personally have approached this Black Death assassin?"

"It appears he was becoming frustrated that your mother survived the assassination on her at your wedding and escaped the raid at that restaurant. It was specifically set up to put her behind bars. He had enough on Zafira to lock her up for the rest of her life."

"Bullshit. We've always made sure Mother is protected. There's nothing out there associating her with the Guzun Bratva."

"There's more to your mother than you realize, Arian. Perhaps, soon, she will disclose her course to you. For now, just believe me when I say, if he had physical proof of what she was about, she would rot in jail."

Arian stared at Bogdan, his eyes turning glacial. "What do you know that I don't, Bogdan?"

"All in due time, Arian. For now, we need to find out what Marek Cermak has against your mother and make sure she stays out of the line of fire."

"I've already instructed Antonio to increase the protection detail at the farm. For now, keep her inside the house at all times, Bogdan."

"Yeah, that's easier said than done," he grumbled.

"Don't think for one moment I'm going to let this go either. You alluded to Mother being involved in something. I want to know what it is. Do you understand?"

"Got it, Pakhan," Bogdan said as he got up and headed to the door, where he stopped and looked at the younger man with a stern expression.

"It's time to make right with Izolda. You know you were wrong, Arian. Be a man, face your fears, and admit why you didn't go after her when she left. Do you honestly think she's safer away from you? Or does it make you feel better about using her the way you did? Yeah... deny it all you want. You used her, in more ways than one. You never apologized for that, Arian." He shook his head.

"Make it right. Be honest. Tell her your fears, but more importantly, tell her your dreams. That's what will tip the scale. Your love and need for her in your life." He held up his hand to stop Arian's protest. "Don't bother denying it. You'll only be fooling yourself."

Bogdan walked out, relieved to notice Arian's shoulders sagging as a sign of acknowledging what he had said. All he could hope for was that he had gotten through to Arian. Izolda and he belonged together. They had loved each other from when they were very young.

"Just like Zafira and I."

The words falling from his lips shook him. He had just preached to Arian while he was rowing the exact same boat.

"Well fuck me," he said as he started the truck. "I guess it's time I took a piece of the pie I dish out and do something about that."

He pulled away in a cloud of dust.

"It's time Ms. Guzun realizes I am the man for her—the only man and the one who will love her until his dying day."

Chapter Sixteen

Penthouse suite, Berd's Hotel, Dimitrie Cantemir Boulevard, Chișinău, Moldova...

"What a surprise, Mr. Guzun." The concierge beamed at Arian, who quickly searched his memory banks since the young man looked familiar. Based on his reaction upon seeing Arian, they must've met before. It didn't take long for him to find the door with the details of when this particular man had appeared in his life.

"Gregory Hamlin, how is your father?"

"You remembered! I didn't think you would; it's been over ten years, and our meeting was so brief," Gregory dragged in a deep breath to calm his excitement. He was clearly in awe of the powerful man in front of him.

"Your father is a good man. If not for his quick action that day, I would've lost my prize bull." Arian winked. "That monster is still around and strutting his stuff on the farm because of your father putting his own life in danger to cut him free from that barbed wire."

"Dad told that story 'til the day of his death two years ago. It was a proud day for him—saving the bull of the man who feeds the hungry all year round in our village."

"It's a small gesture," Arian waved off the praise. "My condolences on his death. How long have you worked here?"

"Three years," Gregory pushed out his chest. "It's temporary while I study law. One more year and I'll be a qualified solicitor."

"Come and see me when that happens, Gregory. We're always looking for young talent in our legal department at AVV Airpro."

"Are you serious, Mr. Guzun?" Gregory's face lit up like a flashlight in a pitch-black night.

"Of course, I am."

"Wow, I can't believe this," he muttered but smiled widely. "I imagine you are here for Mrs. Guzun?"

"Indeed. Is she home?"

"She hardly ever goes out, so, yes. Shall I announce you?"

"I'd like to surprise her, if you don't mind." Arian plastered a sheepish look on his face. "It's time this little tiff between us comes to an end." He leaned closer and whispered conspiratorially, "To be honest, I'm a little nervous. Imagine that, right? The effect a little female could have on a big lug like me."

Gregory laughed. "Indeed, sir. My girlfriend wraps me around her finger every day." He gestured to the elevator on the left. "That one will take you directly up to the penthouse suite level. Good luck, Mr. Guzun."

Arian nodded as the elevator doors closed behind him. It had come as a surprise to find Izolda staying in Moldova. He had thought she would have fled as far away from him as possible.

"Fuck, I'm not ready for this," he muttered as the shudder of the cab indicated it was ascending.

Their marriage never had a chance, especially once he found her on the phone talking to Sanders on their wedding day... right before Zafira was shot. It had been downhill from there. Maybe they might have been able to get past that... except for his actions weeks later...

The last straw for Izolda had been the night when he had cruelly fucked her in front of the mirror.

"*Destul*, I truly messed up that day." He had also told her he had never loved her, that he had only married her to keep her close to find out who was the mastermind in the saga that had been unfolding at the time.

When he had returned from saving Vanya, she was gone. Guilt had kept him from looking for her. It'd been over a year since he had last seen her. That she was still close by filled him with a frisson of hope that perhaps she hadn't come to hate him... much.

Worse, he couldn't blame her if she did. He had treated her in the same callous, ruthless manner Boris Sidorov did—the one thing he had sworn he'd never do.

Still, the knock on the door was firm and confident. The Pakhan of the Guzun Bratva never showed weakness, not even when he felt more vulnerable than ever in his life.

"Give me thirty seconds, then come in," Izolda shouted from inside the suite as the door clicked open. "I just got out of the shower. You can leave the tray on the kitchen counter."

Arian allowed a minute before he entered. The penthouse's sleek, modern design greeted him as he stepped inside—a sanctuary perched high above the bustling city below. The open floor plan flowed seamlessly from one area to the next, bathed in a soft palette of earthy tones and whites that lent an air of sophistication to the space.

Floor-to-ceiling windows stretched along one wall. Beyond the glass, the urban landscape sprawled out in a mesmerizing display of lights and shadows, a reminder of the world below.

"So serene," he murmured as he stood in front of the window. "I wish my life could be like this."

In the center of the room, a plush sectional sofa curved elegantly. Its neutral upholstery blended effortlessly with the surrounding décor, accented by throw pillows in muted tones of taupe and ivory.

Arian's gaze swept across the room, taking in the carefully curated art adorning the walls, the sleek bar that gleamed with polished chrome and glass, and finally, the grand piano standing like a silent sentinel in the corner, its ebony finish contrasting with the lightness of the room. Arian knew Izolda loved playing and could envision the music filling the space, the melodies weaving through the air like whispers of secrets shared in confidence.

His wife had encased herself in a hotel that was more than just a living space—it was a home, a sanctuary, a retreat from the chaos of the world below. Arian turned to stare out to the city below, forcing himself to relax. A tranquility washed over him, a welcome respite from the tension his role as Pakhan of the Guzun Bratva had demanded from him over the past two years of fighting for survival.

"You're not the server from the restaurant."

Arian didn't turn at the soft, melodious voice floating toward him.

"Indeed, I'm not."

"What are you doing here, Arian?"

Arian's eyes locked on the reflection of the woman in the tinted windows. His heart skipped a beat at the sound of her voice, a melody he hadn't heard in far too long. His gaze remained on the reflection of Izolda standing behind him. She was a vision of elegance in her white silk dressing gown, her long blonde hair cascading in soft waves down her back.

For a moment, he simply drank in the sight of her, the memory of her beauty flooding back with an intensity that caught him off guard. He had missed her more than he cared to admit, the ache of her absence a constant companion in the midst of his chaotic world.

As he looked at her reflection in the window, he noticed the subtle tension in her posture, the way she nervously tugged at the knot around her waist. It was a familiar gesture, one that spoke volumes about her unease despite the calm façade she presented.

"You are the last person I expected to see here," she murmured in a voice barely above a whisper.

Their eyes met in the reflection, her expression unreadable. "And yet here I am," he replied. The hint of sadness and regret that tinged his tone rang in his ears. His lips compressed, but he still didn't move.

Arian felt a pang of guilt stab at his heart. At that moment, as he stood facing her, he couldn't deny the rush of emotion that surged through him at the sight of her.

"Again..." Her voice was clipped this time, as if she wanted to run but couldn't make her legs obey her brain. "What are you doing here, Arian?"

"I missed you." The echo of the words spilling out before he could stop them mocked him. The way she startled in surprise pushed him to continue. "More than I thought possible."

Finally turning to face her, he was relieved to notice Izolda's expression softening at his words, and her eyes held a glimmer of warmth that stirred something deep within him. They stood silently, bathed in the soft glow of the city lights and in that moment, Arian knew that despite everything, he had finally found his way back to her.

Now, he had to convince her of his love and pray she could find it in her heart to forgive him and come back home.

"What about me do you miss, Arian? Oh, wait, I remember… it's the convenient fuck holes that your conjugal rights give you to use when the need demands it." Her eyes glimmered with painful remembrance. "Or is my recollection of events wrong?"

"Regret always comes too late, doesn't it?" he murmured in a low voice. "I never apologized to you for that…" He grimaced. "Or for all the other fuck ups I played a part in that formed your life's path."

"You weren't responsible for everything that went wrong in my life, Arian."

"Wasn't I?" He shrugged. "Maybe not directly, but everything that happened to you from the day you met me was because of our love for each other.

Yes, I didn't know why you married Boris, but it did break my heart. Of course, in true Arian Guzun fashion, I didn't find you to talk about it. I turned my back on you. Over time, my feelings turned to hatred for Boris... for you, and that was what guided my actions toward you.

"I couldn't accept that you hadn't trusted me with what Boris threatened you with. That you believed me too weak to protect you and your parents. It hurt, Izolda... it showed you never trusted me—the one thing I gave you unconditionally all those years ago, and you threw it back in my face."

"Arian, it was so much more complicated than that."

"Was it?" Arian watched her unblinkingly for long moments. The deep sigh came from years of questioning himself, his actions, and his beliefs about why he hadn't been good enough for her. Even though he now knew the truth, the pain he had carried all these years was still like a ghost roaming the devil's realm, searching for a way out.

"I lied."

"I know." Izolda didn't have to ask; they both knew what he was referring to.

"Then why did you leave?"

"Because you didn't realize it then. That night... the way you forced yourself on me... I couldn't stay because I knew eventually being treated like that would break me and kill any chance we had of ever finding our way back to each other." She smiled at his expression. "It would have, Arian, because no matter how badly you treat me, the moment you touch me, I melt. I can never deny you, even the times I hate how cheap you made me feel. You are in my blood, my soul, and my heart. Why do you think I'm still here in Moldova?"

"Izolda..." Arian's voice cracked as he walked closer. The shock in her eyes was profound as he knelt and took her hands in his. For the mighty Pakhan of the Guzun Bratva to be in such a subjugating position was something no one would believe. "I came here to beg for forgiveness, and here you are, making me feel ten feet tall. If anything, you should hate me and chase me out."

"That was my initial intention until you turned around, and I saw the regret in your eyes, the warmth and the love begging to be set free." She cupped his cheeks and leaned down to briefly kiss his lips. "I can never hate you, Arian. I love you. I always have, and God help me, I always will."

"As I love you, my beautiful wife... and if you'd let me, I am going to take the rest of the night to prove it to you."

"Demanding your conjugal rights again, Mr. Guzun?"

"No, my love... begging you to let me love you with my heart and soul, using my body as the conduit to portray all my regrets and future intentions." Pressing his face into her soft belly, his arms circled her waist. "I love you, Izolda Guzun and I can't go on without you in my life. Please, release me from the hell I've been living the past year with your absence."

"Then show me, Arian... let's open the gates of hell and release you from that prison into the light of love."

Arian picked her up and carried her to the bedroom, his expression relaxed and unburdened for the first time in his adult life.

They quickly became lost in a mutual raw passion that was in complete contrast to the gentle touch of his hands and the promise of unbound pleasure in his eyes.

The world fell away as their bodies reunited in a blend of passion, desire, and unconditional love.

Afterward, their ragged breathing quieting down, Arian hugged her against his chest. With eyes closed, he held her, savoring her essence soaking through his skin.

Finally, he felt at peace. He was home.

Gently cupping her chin, he tilted her head back and kissed her in a meshing of warmth, passion, and need. The same bond they had formed the moment their eyes had met so many years ago.

"Thank you, my dearest wife, for setting me free. Now, our future can finally begin."

Izolda returned his smile as she pressed her fingers against his chest, where his heart beat rapidly.

Linzi Basset

"Our future... I like the sound of that."

Chapter Seventeen

GUZUN
BRATVA

A week later, Ferma La Guzun...

"I'm surprised Bogdan isn't hogging your private space as usual," Vanya quipped as she joined Zafira in the sunroom of her mansion.

"I chased him off. Sent him to exercise my horse since I'm not allowed to ride." Zafira snorted delicately. "Why I even allow that Goliath to order me around is beyond me."

"Really? Do you want me to spell it out for you?"

"Vanya, stop. I already told you, I am not in love with Bogdan Rusu."

"Hmm." Vanya selected a sandwich from the tray on the coffee table and sat back. "You do know there's a difference between being in love and loving someone, right?"

Zafira pressed her lips together. Her daughter was too forward and too persistent. Once she caught wind of something, she wouldn't let go until she was satisfied with the outcome.

"Drop it, my darling. I refuse to become one of the projects you need to fix. The relationship between Bogdan and me is beyond that. In fact, it was torn apart before it truly began."

"Do tell!" She finished the sandwich and picked up a chocolate croissant. Biting into it, she sighed heavenly, "Ohh, this is sooo good." Glancing at Zafira, she prodded, "You know I'm not gonna stop, so you might as well tell me the dirty tale."

"It doesn't put Bogdan in a good light, Vanya, and I know how much you love and respect him, so let's just drop it, please."

"Now I'm even more intrigued. C'mon, Mother, spill the beans!"

"We were in love. It was inevitable but my parents and the Guzuns had struck a deal that your father and I should marry. We were the perfect match to form a Bratva allegiance between the two families. Unfortunately, Bogdan was the one my heart wanted. My parents refused to listen to reason and continued to make wedding arrangements. On our wedding day, I put my foot down and pleaded with them to understand my love for another and why I couldn't marry Viktor. My father showed me a check stub where he had paid Bogdan off to forget about me."

"A check stub means shit, and you know it."

"My mother confirmed that she had seen the cleared check. The fact that Bogdan wasn't at the wedding, even though he was Viktor's best man, was the only reason I went along with the marriage. It was the only confirmation I needed that he had taken the money. His love for me was worth a measly ten million rubles."

"That's bullshit." Vanya jumped up and turned on Zafira. "Did you even bother to look into what Andrei said about Bogdan inheriting the duke's title and entire estate?"

"Yes," Zafira admitted with a crestfallen look. "It doesn't change anything. Secrets like those were what had destroyed the trust we supposedly had. Don't you see that?"

"No, Mother, what I see is a woman refusing to admit she made a mistake in believing her parents, even after all these years. Bogdan inherited billions two years before Granddad offered him that money. You know as well as I do that wealth never held meaning to him. If it did, why would he have lived a life of an underling to Dad? I'll tell you why." She stabbed a finger in the air. "Because he loved you, and he knew the day would come that you would need protection." Her voice lowered. "And you did, didn't you? All those years, that's how you coped living with a man you never truly loved… because the one who did own your heart was by your side every day, protecting your life as much as your heart."

"What was that?" Zafira's head jerked at the dull popping sounds coming from the patio where Antonio and two guards kept watch. She ran to the window and cautiously peered out. Two of the guards were lying in a pool of blood. Antonio was hunched behind a large concrete pot plant. He furiously gestured for her to get out of sight while he made a phone call. "*Blyad*! They've been shot. Get to the study. Run, Vanya! Go, now."

Vanya didn't ask questions but sprinted down the hallway to the study, where their escape route was waiting for them. Viktor had ensured the house was prepared for situations like these, and a shadow wall leading to an underground tunnel offered them safety.

Another volley of shots from the front of the house echoed through the hallway, followed by the crash of the front door giving way under a heavy boot.

"They're inside. Get into the tunnel and run. You know where the safe house is. Get to it and phone for help."

"I'm not leaving you behind, Mom. Come, we need to—"

Zafira caught her hands. "No, my darling. It's my duty to keep you safe, and it's your duty to keep your children safe. That's what's important now. Think of your unborn children. Go. I'll keep them off as long as I can. Hopefully, Antonio managed to get hold of Bogdan, and he's on his way."

"Be safe, *Mamochka*." Vanya hugged her fiercely. "Your grandchildren are going to need their nana around."

"Go!" Zafira urged as the soft footfall ascending the stairs warned her the perpetrators were close. "*Slava Bogu*." With a sigh of relief, she watched Vanya disappear through the hidden door in the corner of the room. When the shadow of the assassin darkened the doorway, Zafira was ready. Her stance was perfect, calm, confident, and unwavering as she lifted the Glock and took aim.

"I hate uninvited guests," she sneered as she squeezed the trigger. By the time the man's head turned in her direction, it was too late. The bullet slammed into the door behind him, splattering brain matter and blood as the bullet drilled a path through his skull. When his body hit the floor, he was already dead.

"I swear, Luciano Maranzano, when I get my hands on you, I'm gonna squeeze you like the low-life bug you are," Vanya sneered as she quickly crawled along the narrow space in pitch-black darkness. She knew these tunnels all by heart since she had played in them ad nauseum when she was little. Except danger had never chased her, and now the short distance to the stairway leading to the underground tunnels seemed miles away.

"God, please keep my mother safe. She's too young to die," she murmured as she fumbled for her cell phone and switched on the flashlight. Maneuvering the uneven stairs in the dark was dangerous, and she refused to put her unborn children's lives in more danger by being overly cautious.

Vanya hated running from a fight, more so leaving her mother behind to battle alone, but Zafira had been right. The only thought that had been running through her mind from the moment the first gunshot had sounded was to protect her twins.

"Don't worry, poppets. Mommy isn't going to die today because Daddy will be seriously pissed if I do, so... we're gonna do this together." She hesitated to open the steel door when she reached the outside latch two miles from the house on the far side of a rocky hill. "*Blyad*! What are the chances that someone is waiting on the outside for me?"

Vanya depended on her ever-present sixth sense cautioning her against storming out blindly. There were guards all over the farm and still a group of assassins managed to bypass them to get to the house. Clearly, there were some corrupt members on their team. Vanya flinched at the echo of a shot coming from the study but refused to give way to the fear that her mother might be dead.

"She has survived two attacks. This time, she knew they were coming and was ready. I have to believe that. Mom isn't dead!" Vanya checked her phone. "*Blyad*! No signal," she muttered as she keyed in the access code that would unlock the latch. "Well, poppets, we can't stay here. If there are more of them, they'll find the hidden door at some point. Just go to sleep. Mommy's got this."

Vanya's heart pounded wildly as she cautiously pushed open the latch of the underground tunnel's exit. With every creak, her fear intensified, her mind racing with the thought of the danger lurking just beyond. But she couldn't afford to hesitate; her instincts urged her forward, driven by a fierce maternal determination to protect her unborn children.

Stepping out into the open air, Vanya squinted against the sudden brightness of the day. Before her stretched a vast expanse of grassy hillside, rolling gently beneath the azure sky. In the distance, the patchwork quilt of farmlands spread out like a painting, a tranquil scene that belied the turmoil raging within her.

Though the landscape was serene, Vanya's senses remained on high alert, and every nerve tingled with trepidation. She couldn't discount that danger lurked in the shadows, that every step she took could be her last, but she refused to let fear paralyze her. Instead, it fueled her determination to keep her children safe at all costs.

"Don't worry," she exhaled slowly and repeated the words, more to calm herself than anything else, "Mommy's got this."

Resolutely, she scanned the immediate area for any sign of trouble. Her back snapped ramrod straight as a familiar mocking voice sounded from atop the grassy knoll where she stood just outside the tunnel entrance.

"One thing I have to give the Guzuns. If nothing else, you are predictable as fuck."

By the time she turned to face him, Luciano Maranzano stood an arm's length from her. Hatred for the man threatened to choke her, but she forced a smirk on her face.

"Well, I can't say it's a pleasure seeing you again, fuckface." Acting irresponsibly wasn't an option, but that didn't mean she had to be polite. Still, it would be prudent to be cautious. This man had no empathy and wouldn't care that she was pregnant.

"Careful, *la mia bella donna*. I might just believe you missed me."

"I'm not your anything, you demented, dickless, piece of shit— Ugh!"

Vanya realized it was the worst thing she could've said as the black claws of unconsciousness wrapped around her before the pain of the gun smashed against the back of her head penetrated. The words he sneered accompanied her drifting off into the dark void of nothingness.

"You fucking bitch… you're gonna pay for that."

Linzi Basset

Zafira

Chapter Eighteen

Three days later, Ferma La Guzun...

"You will finish this plate of food today, even if I have to force it down your throat," Bogdan's growl resonated ominously through the room. "You barely eat enough to sustain your body."

"Stop mothering me, Rusu. I don't need a keeper," Zafira snapped as she studied the CCTV footage that was routed to her laptop. The IT team had installed facial recognition software and although they were scouring the web 24/7 for signs of Vanya and Maranzano, she insisted on doing it herself.

"What you need is sustenance and rest. You're no good to anyone in this state, *Comare*, least of all your daughter."

"My daughter is in this mess because of me." She turned on him with fury flashing from her eyes. A fist bumped her chest. "Me! Do you hear me? It's my fault that she's missing."

"No, Zafira," Bogdan said gently. "Maranzano's gripe is with Andrei and what he did to him a year ago. It's him he wants to punish. That the rest of us suffer alongside him is a bonus in his warped mind."

"That might be, but my gut instinct tells me someone else is behind this. You forget I've been the target all along. The assassinations have all been aimed at me. Maranzano might want vengeance on Vanya and Andrei, but there's something else afoot. I just don't know what." A frown creased her brow. "You never got around telling me why we had to leave Czechia so quickly."

"Triska and Marek Cermak aren't who they seem, Zafira. Vanya came across content on the dark web that alluded to an association between them, Seymon Mochilevich, and Artem Melnyk."

Zafira turned rigid. "What do you mean by alluding to an association? What kind of connection did you find, Bogdan?"

"It involves a coup d'etat of the *Novaya Volna* Group, more specifically eliminating their leader, the Shadow Don, aka… you, Zafira."

"Are you saying that they want to become involved with the Bratva's New Order? That they're aware of my family running the Guzun Bratva Group?"

"Indeed, they are."

"How? No one knows—not even Seymon or Artem. Guzun is such a common name in the EU, which is why no one ever questioned or suspected us."

"Because you are such successful business entrepreneurs and support the poor in the community. You've covered all the tracks that could lead to suspicion, but somehow, the Cermaks found a loophole."

"I still don't understand. Marek is the First Vice President of the Czech Republic. He stands the chance of becoming the next president, so why compromise the career he has built all his life? He turned to politics soon after their daughter Azja was born. You have to be mistaken, Bogdan. He doesn't have a corrupt bone in his body."

"Most people will say the same about you and your family, Zafira. He knows you managed to live a double life. Maybe that's the kind of untapped control he's after as well."

Zafira got up. "If what you say is true, it means he's working with Maranzano, and Vanya was taken to draw me out." Her eyes flashed dangerously. "No matter their age, only a coward uses children in their quest for power. So, since I'm such an accommodating woman, let's give him what he wants, Bogdan—me in exchange for Vanya."

"Zafira, let's not act in haste. I'm speculating at best and—"

"Show me."

Bogdan knew it would be best to arm her with as much knowledge as possible, so it was amusing to listen to his muttering of "hardheaded woman" while he logged into his network using her laptop.

With growing trepidation, she quickly scanned and read the various folders Vanya had compiled.

"This is beyond speculation, Bogdan. This is proof that Marek Cermak has been involved and pocketing gains from the Solntvesoka Bratva for over twenty years. In fact, reading between the lines, I'd say he's the one in charge and not Artem Melnyk."

"Exactly the conclusion Vanya and I made."

"You should've told me this sooner. Now, we're fighting from the back foot!"

"We began this fight trailing behind since their onslaught against us began, Zafira. Only it took us this long to realize it. We've been fighting the most obvious enemy while the unknown was hiding in clear sight behind a trusted fealty of yours."

"I find it hard to believe that he would go to such lengths purely for power, Bogdan. No," she tapped a nail against her teeth as she pondered the situation. "There's more to this than meets the eye."

"Maybe, but never discount how being invisible adds to the lure of a criminal. You should know that feeling better than anyone."

"You were always against what I was doing with the Novaya Volna Group. I never understood why. You're the only one who knows the real reason why I began the New Order Bratva movement."

"To honor your father and revive his legacy that Viktor had tainted in his final years. Yes, I know, but in the process, you placed a big, red target on your back, Zafira. More so... you put all your children's lives at risk."

Zafira turned pale. She couldn't dispute what he said, but she refused to acknowledge the truth of it. The decision to form a coalition with Bratva groups eager for change and a modern outlook to evolving criminal enterprises was the right one. She had come too far and given up too much to walk away from it now. The end was in sight. The New Bratva Order of Novaya Volna would rule over all... with her as their Shadow Don.

No one was going to stand in her way. Not Marek Cermak, Bogdan Rusu, or even... her own children.

Resolutely squaring her shoulders, she chose not to debate the issue further and said in a clipped tone, "You can accompany me or stay, but I'm going to the Chez Republic, Rusu."

"Very well, but heed my warning, Zafira. Maranzano doesn't yield to any man. In his eyes, he has all the power. He's not going to give up his revenge on an order from Cermak, of that I have no doubt."

"I'll take care of Cermak, so I guess it'll be up to you to make sure my daughter and our grandchildren don't get hurt in the process." Tossing her head in defiance as he opened his mouth to protest, she walked toward the stairs. "Enough. Get ahold of Arian and Andrei and update them. I prefer they all accompany us. We've always had more strength as one family unit. I want to be on the way within the hour."

"We're in the air, so where exactly are we going, Zafira? It serves no purpose to arrive at Cermak's house without a well-thought-out plan. All we'll achieve is endangering Vanya's life." Bogdan refused to cower in the face of Zafira's glare.

"Bogdan is right," Arian said. "If we go to his house, he'll be sure to use it to his benefit. We don't want to give him more ways to increase his popularity with the public. Yes, we're all in agreement that he has control of the Solntvesoka Bratva and that Seymon Mochilevich, Artem Melnyk, and probably many other syndicate leaders are under his power, but we have to be clever about our approach. If we fail, we might not find Vanya, and he will gain more power than any single person should have in the criminal empire."

"So, what do we do, Arian?" Zafira paced the cabin. "It's been days, and there have been no demands for Vanya's release. That means only one thing—they want us to fall apart."

Zafira

"And once we do, we'll be vulnerable," Vadim interjected quietly. "They have no fucking idea who they're dealing with, do they?"

"Calm down, honey," said his wife, Sabira. "Anger isn't going to achieve anything. We need to strategize."

"Sabira is right." Andrei hadn't said a word for days. He had been searching longer and harder than anyone else. The black circles under his eyes were proof that he hadn't slept much since Vanya had been taken. "Vanya is clever. She knows Maranzano better than anyone. She'll stay alert and keep out of trouble, but we have to get to her… sooner rather than later. That Sicilian bastard is unpredictable. We know Cermak is involved." He looked at Zafira. "Phone him. Ask him bald-faced what he wants."

Bogdan mulled over Andrei's suggestion. "It has merit, and it will put a damper on his initial plan of playing emotional mind games with us. He will have to regroup and meet with Maranzano, so let's wait until we're in Prague before you call him, Zafira. The closer we are to him, the quicker we can react."

"Catch him off guard, in other words," Zafira agreed with a nod. "How long before we land, Arian?"

"Forty-five minutes. The private airstrip is a ten-minute drive from Kramář's Villa. I've already asked our IT team to send one of our drones to the Villa and confirm the Cermak's presence. If they're not there, our plan will fall apart."

"Good. Wake me when we're about to land. I need to think." Zafira summarily closed her eyes, and within seconds, she was asleep. It was one of the perks she had learned over time. To completely switch off and drift off quickly. Short naps like these were powerful and just what she needed at present.

The last thoughts milling through her mind weren't centered on their current mission. No, it was directed at Bogdan and how sleeping gave her a reason not to look at him. The dratted man had been unsettling her more and more the past couple of weeks with his brooding stares and expressive eyes.

Exactly! Since when does the master of stoicism show his feelings? It's like he's stamping his ownership over me with every glance.

What concerned her even more was that the thought of belonging to him filled her with thrilling expectations. There was no doubt he was a powerful Dominant, a fact he had proved more than once. The way he made her lose control and guided what her body craved without her realizing it confirmed what she had always known—Bogdan was more in tune with her needs than Viktor had ever been.

Not just my needs… he knows—I'm sure he has figured out—that I still love him. With a start, she came to a realization—that was why he had stayed all these years. Maybe it was time she opened her heart and stopped blaming him for things he had no control over. *Not maybe—it's time, period. I need him in my life. I know it, and God help me, so does he.*

Linzi Basset

Zafira

Chapter Nineteen

An hour later, two minutes out from Kramář's Vilia, Prague, Chez Republic...

"So, you finally decided to call and apologize for running out on us in the middle of the night," Marek Cermak answered Zafira's call on the fourth ring.

"*Basta con le stronzate*, Marek. We both know why I'm phoning."

"Cut the crap you say. As always, straight to the point. I've always been impressed with your ability to curse in every language." A short silence followed as Marek considered what Zafira knew. "I'm a lot of things, Zafira, but I'm not a psychic, so I'm incapable of reading your mind. Let's not waste each other's time, and tell me why you're phoning."

"You have my daughter, you sonofabitch, but what I don't know is why. Why her... and why me?"

Zafira's body trembled with suppressed anger. She had been living a double life since birth, but to be on the receiving end of similar deceit was infuriating, especially since she had believed Triska and Marek were real friends of the family. It didn't matter that he had criminal intentions. Hell, she was the epitome of a Bratva regime and all the blackness that came along with it, but they had shunned the closeness they had built up through the years... that hit her hard.

"Come now, Zafira. Surely you know better than to ask me that... or what am I saying, Shadow Don?"

"Shadow Don?" Arian murmured questioningly at Bogdan. Everyone had heard of the covert New Order Bratva group headed up by a powerful and very rich person. Zafira shot a warning glare at Bogdan. Of course, her children were too sharp not to catch on. "*Isus Hristos!*" Everyone echoed Arian's shocked expression as he stared at her. "You're the Shadow Don?"

"Ah, tut-tut-tut, *Comare*, keeping secrets from the family, are you? What I'd like to know is how that Hercules hogging your heels knew about me before you did? It was him who made you leave that night, wasn't it?"

"*Accidenti, giusto, bastardo*," Bogdan sneered. "You're not as clever at staying under the radar as you believed. Once I smelled a rat, I didn't stop until I found the fucking stink that you're hiding under."

"So eloquently put, Mr. Rusu. I'd be careful if I was you. I have enough on you to have you incarcerated for life."

"As I do you, fuckface."

Marek went quiet, clearly put out by Bogdan's response.

"Yeah, threats don't work on me. Now, where the fuck is Vanya?"

"Are you out of your mind, Marek? Put the phone down! You know the risk of having such a conversation here." The voice of Triska Cermak sounded muffled over the phone.

"This is an encrypted line, Triska, and stop fucking telling me what to do."

"Put that phone down. We need to go before that asshole you're working with does something stupid and eliminates the only advantage we have over that bitch." Zafira flinched as Triska's words echoed through the cab of the van, which Vadim had just brought to a stop around the corner from Kramář's Villa.

"I'm warning you, Marek, if Luciano Maranzano hurts one hair on my daughter's head, you won't see the sun rising in the morning."

"Your daughter is alive, that's all I can say, and if you wish her to remain as such, you will refrain from making any further insults or threats. You forget who and what I am, Zafira Guzun."

"Do I? Quite frankly, Marek Cermak, I don't believe I even know who you are."

"What you need to realize is that I am a very powerful man, *Comare*. Not only here in the Chez Republic but all across the EU. As soon as I am elected as the president, my reach will increase tenfold. Then I will be untouchable. I suggest you sit back and relax. The election is two weeks away. Do exactly as I say, and your little Vanya will come out of this rosy-eyed and bushy-tailed. If not... well, you do know Maranzano hates every one of you now..."

"What do you mean, do as you say? What the fuck do you want from me, Marek?"

"All in due time, my dear. For now, I believe I have an appointment with your arch-enemy. *Laters*, Ms. Guzun," he said in a sardonic chuckle before ending the call.

"Our respective teams are ready to track whatever vehicles leave the compound via three different satellites and two overhead drones," Arian said to assure Zafira they wouldn't lose sight of the Cermaks.

"I'll stay out of sight, but we will know exactly where they go," Vadim interjected. "At least we know they're on their way to meet that useless Sicilian."

"Finally, we'll have that motherfucker." Andrei's voice was ominous as he looked at Arian. "This time, you won't stop me. Maranzano touched Vanya for the last time."

"You'll have to get in line." Arian's voice sounded dark and evil in the narrow confines of the van. "It's because of my judgment error that he once again terrorized my sister. I will be the one to end his miserable life."

Two miles outside of Chýně, Prague-West District, Central Bohemian Region of the Czech Republic...

"You're fucked, you know." Vanya had been mocking Luciano non-stop from the moment they had arrived at the remote farmhouse just outside of Prague. It was a wonder he hadn't backhanded her yet. She snorted at the thought. Even if he had wanted to, he wouldn't be able to since he had locked her in a cage. *Stupid asshole.* "I might be the one locked inside this cage, but you're the beast trapped within the steel bars of your past. I always thought you were clever, but it seems I was mistaken."

"Keep your fucking trap shut. I'm tired of listening to your teeming voice all day long."

"Come now, darling, isn't that why I'm here? To keep you entertained since you're too stupid to unchain yourself from the past?" She stretched out her long legs, as if she was sitting on a chaise lounge next to a swimming pool in the Caribbean. "One would think you've learned your lesson by now." She chuckled. "Can you imagine what Andrei has in store for you? Tsk-tsk, Luciano, you really didn't think this through, did you? I mean, he cut off your already teeny weeny dick for your measly attempt to rape me. Can you imagine what he's going to do now that you took me and his unborn children from him? Ahh, I can't wait. It's going to be better than the goriest horror movie I've ever watched!"

"*Quindi aiutami Dio*, if you don't fucking shut up, I'm going to sew your lips together."

"Well, you can try, but I promise you, that needle is going to end up so far up your ass, it's going to feel like you've swallowed a toothpick that got stuck sideways in your throat."

Vanya was sick and tired of the horrid conditions of the barn. She had no idea where they were since Luciano had spiked the water he had forced her to drink when she came to. She also had no idea how long she had been unconscious, so she couldn't even try to ascertain her location. Her worst fear when she had woken up was that whatever he had given her had hurt her babies, but that threat was soon laid to rest. The twins had started moving and were very active, most probably more so since she didn't move around and felt every little ripple they caused. It was hot and humid, and she reeked of sweat. The t-shirt and jeans stuck to her body. If not for the once-feared Mafia mobster leering at her all the time, she would be tempted to take them off.

"For a woman in your position, you have a lot to say. I've got news for you, slut. No one knows where you are, and we made sure this place is secure. They'll never find you. I was careful to avoid every public camera out there. Yeah, I know all your Guzun tricks. Hacking into the satellite feeds and the GeoEye system. Well, none of that's gonna work."

Vanya startled as he slammed a hand against the cage, rattling it wildly.

"You're mine now, bitch." His eyes glimmered like a psycho about to commit murder. "You and those brats you're carrying. Yes." He laughed at her expression. "Once they're born, you will have served your purpose. Then I'll post your corpse back to your dear husband, but those babies… they'll be mine. I'm the one they'll call Papa, and I'll be the one kissing them goodnight before bed. Ah, such pleasure vengeance brings, don't you agree?"

"You're not just an idiot. You are completely demented." Vanya did her best not to show the fear his words awakened inside her. If what he said was true and he kept her locked in here for the next four months, no one would be able to find her.

"No, my dear little bitch, I am finally going to get what I've been dreaming about all my life. To have the money, the power, and the family I wanted. With the backing I'll have going forward, nothing and no one will stand in my way. I'm going to rule the world."

"Dream on, fuckface," she snickered as she leaned her head back against the steel bars. It was uncomfortable, to say the least. The solid steel slave cage was high enough for her to sit up but too short for her to lie down and straighten her legs. Still, she refused to show Luciano the effect his words had on her. "If you think I'm going to sit around and wait for someone to come and save me, you don't know me very well."

Luciano burst out laughing. "Now, who's dreaming? I'm never unlocking that cage, bitch. Even the doctor coming to examine you will do so through the bars. The only time it'll be unlocked is the moment those brats are ready to pop out and only to allow you to lie down to give birth." He smirked evilly. "Half in and half out of the cage is as far as you'll go. As soon as they're out, you'll be locked up again."

"You better hope you didn't leave any crumbs out there, Maranzano, because if you did, my family will find it."

"I suggest you start showing me respect, or I'll be forced to deny you the luxury of the amenities you currently have. If not for the stench I would have to endure, I would enjoy you being covered in your own piss and shit."

Vanya didn't respond but flinched within herself at the appalling vision his words painted. Maranzano was teetering on the brink of total psychosis. If she wasn't terrified for the lives of her babies, she would push him over, but since she had no idea how he would react, she had to curb the instinct to keep taunting him.

"Be my guest. I don't give a shit one way or the other." Ignoring him, she tilted her head back and closed her eyes. "They... who are they?"

"What are you blabbering about now?" Maranzano eyed her through narrowed lids.

"You said that no one knows where I am and that *we* made sure this place is secure. Just who the fuck is behind my abduction, shit face?"

"I guess I shouldn't be surprised that your mouth is as filthy as your mother's." The voice sounding from the doorway shook Vanya to the core.

"Marek Cermak and... Triska... what is the meaning of this?" She shook her head to clear her mind. Yes, she had found information linking them to the Czech and Russian Bratva groups, but she would never have believed they would hurt her or be in cahoots with the likes of Luciano Maranzano. She and their daughter, Azja, were best friends.

"What the fuck are you doing here?" Luciano's irritation was evident in his grating voice.

Vanya knew it was a sign that he hated his authority being usurped. Clearly, there was a power play going on here.

"I thought we agreed that you would stay away. What if the Guzuns are watching you?"

"They're not, so you can relax." Marek stared at Vanya. "A cage, Luciano? Is that really necessary?"

"Keep out of this. We discussed this on your boat. You wanted to draw Zafira Guzun out, and I set in play a way to get her here. Your and my objectives were achieved by taking this bitch. What I do with her is my business. You just cast the bait when you're ready, and the *Comare* will come running.

"Yeah... except she's not gonna wait for any of you to throw the line." Vanya smiled gaily as the three people looked at her. "It seems you don't know my mother as well as you thought, Mr. Cermak... See, my mother is a much better fisherman than you."

Zafira

Chapter Twenty

"Get her out of that fucking cage, Andrei." Zafira's voice sounded foreign, filled with fury that threatened to bubble over from finding her beautiful daughter filthy and underfed, locked in a steel cage like a wild animal. The gun in her hand was steady as she aimed it at the three people. "I suggest none of you move. I wouldn't think twice about pulling this trigger. *Blyad'*! She can't even stand," Zafira's resolve threatened to collapse as she watched Andrei catch Vanya when her legs crumbled the moment she attempted to stand.

"You heard the Comare," Bogdan growled as Marek Cermak's hand crept toward his waist. "She might shoot, but I won't think twice about ripping your fucking head from your body."

"You better listen to the big guy," Luciano smirked. "He's been sniffing at the Guzuns asses his whole life and doesn't make idle threats."

"Something you seem to have forgotten, fuckface," Arian sneered. "We all warned you what would happen if you ever came near Vanya again. It seems the year you spent in exile dulled your memory."

"Baby, are you okay?" Zafira's voice quivered. Her attention was now solely on her daughter, but she had full confidence in Bogdan and her sons to protect them from further harm.

"I'm fine, *Mamochka.* This dickless Sicilian mobster isn't likely to ever get the better of me. I've been indulging him to keep my babies safe. Otherwise, I would've kicked his nut sack up his ass a long time ago."

"That's my girl," Zafira sniffed away the tears that burned behind her eyelids at the sight of her bedraggled daughter. Her gaze shifted to the three people in front of them. "So, who's got the guts to spill the beans?" She walked closer, aware of Bogdan hugging her side to keep watch over her.

Zafira

"You're the First Vice President of the Czech Republic, Marek. We've been friends for as long as our daughters have been alive. Never in all those years have you shown any sign of resentment toward me or my family."

"Your family. Now see… there's the kicker, Zafira. YOUR family," Marek sneered with hatred spitting venom from his eyes. "You have everything. Money, power. You grew up in the lap of luxury while I suffered in poverty, abuse, and hunger."

"I am hardly to blame for how you grew up, Marek."

"Oh, but you are to blame… my dear big sis!"

"What the fuck!?" Vadim and Arian growled simultaneously.

"You didn't know? I'm not surprised she never told you. See, your mother is one of twins."

"We know that, but her brother died a couple of hours after childbirth."

"Died? Hardly, my dear boy… since here I am. Alive and well."

"I don't understand," Zafira was as confused as her children. "This is… you're lying. This is nothing other than a bullshit story. You're nothing to me. My brother is dead."

"Our dear mother, before she took her final breath, bless her black soul, admitted it all to me, so no, it's not a bullshit story."

"What do you mean before she took her final breath?" Zafira struggled to remain calm. Her mother had been brutally murdered twenty years ago, but the authorities had caught the murderer. A young drug addict who had broken into her house in search of money to feed his habit—or so she had been made to believe.

"Because I was there. I finally found out the truth when the woman I grew up believing to be my mother died. Since she was dying, she didn't fear repercussions from Agata Solovyov and told me what had happened that day. Yes, she was the nurse who was saddled with the son your mother didn't want. Our dear father was furious when you popped out ahead of me since, as you know, the firstborn was his successor. That he would have to hand his legacy over to a woman infuriated him. He forced everyone to claim otherwise. That I was the firstborn. Agata hated him for that. In her eyes, it was deception of the worst kind, and she refused to let it go. She gave me away... like a useless toy.

"She handed me to one of the nurses and forgot about me. All because she was a feminist who believed women had as much right as men in the world of the Bratva." He snorted. "That decision cost her dearly. Did you know..." His eyes glimmered darkly. "She was my first kill and, to date, the most rewarding."

"You killed your own mother?" Vanya's voice sounded teary as the past couple of weeks finally caught up with her, and she started crying.

"She killed me first by giving me away, then forgetting I was ever born," Marek sneered. "Denied me what was rightfully mine! For that, she had to pay, and now... it's your turn, my dear sister."

"Is that why you went to Moldova at the time of Azja's birth? I suppose our meeting was well-planned." Zafira shook her head sadly.

"No, it wasn't, since I didn't know at the time we were family, but you interfered with our plans for our future when you rushed Triska to the hospital, even though you were already in labor."

"I don't understand."

"We never wanted children," Triska interjected. Her lips were pressed into a grim line. "I wasn't mother material, and just thinking of wasting time on a being that stuck to me like a parasite revolted me."

"I felt the same," Marek continued. "The intention was to give the brat away to a poor family in Chişinău, but because of you and Viktor's status in Moldova, the tabloids had a field day with your bravery. We had no choice but to keep the child to save face. You fucked up our plans to build the Bratva family business we had just begun at that point. Because of all the exposure, I was thrown into the world of politics and a career I hated with a passion."

"And that's why you want me dead?"

"*Isus Hristos*, you're a fucked up bastard," Vadim interjected.

"Shut your mouth, you prick. I'm superior to you, and you will show me respect!" Marek shouted.

His eyes glowed like fireballs that gave him the look of an evil monster about to explode.

Vadim snorted. "Demanding my respect? You truly are demented. My parents taught us that respect has to be earned, and no matter your position in life or that you're my supposed uncle, you don't deserve an ounce of reverence from any of us."

"Oh, for fuck's sake. This drivel is making me want to puke," Luciano growled. He was visually furious that his plans had once again been foiled. "Let's finish this, once and for all."

"Are you proposing a medieval dual, fuckface?" Bogdan mocked him as he gestured around. "Since we outnumber and outgun you two to one."

"Except you don't," the voice behind them had barely slammed against the wood-slatted walls when two gunshots shattered the silence.

"*La dracu!*" Vadim cursed as one of the bullets drilled a path through his side to slam into the wall behind him. Luckily for him, he had spun around when Svetlana Rebane's voice penetrated his mind; otherwise, the bullet would've paralyzed him.

"You useless bitch!" Vanya screamed as she watched her brother drop to the dirt floor. Before Andrei could stop her, she catapulted herself toward the redhead, flattening her with a vicious dropkick to the jaw. "No one fucking hurts my brothers except for me. Do you hear me? No one!"

"Still as feisty as ever, isn't she?" Marek said drily as he moved quicker than Bogdan could anticipate and caught Zafira in a chokehold. "I suggest you let go of my sister, Vanya, or your mother is going to taste lead, which is going to piss me off to no end since I have a much more painful death in mind for her." A hedonistic laugh escaped from his chest as he caught Bogdan and Arian's movements. "I wouldn't if I was you." He looked at his sister, who was struggling to her feet, still groggy from the brutal kick against her jaw. "Well? Do you need help, or can you get your fucking gun and take charge of your troops?"

"Fuck off, Marek," she sneered, picking up the shiny silver pistol from the ground. "Anyone moves, shoot them," she instructed the four men flanking her. With venom spitting from her eyes, she looked at Vanya. "Except for that bitch. She's mine. I intend to make her bleed before she dies."

Linzi Basset

Zafira

Chapter Twenty-One

For moments, silence descended on the group as they became wrapped in a cocoon of tension. It didn't last long. It couldn't, and no one knew it better than Bogdan. He knew how quickly a situation like this could escalate and turn upside down.

"You made one miscalculation, Cermak," he taunted Marek. He showed no concern for Svetlana and her men but kept his eyes glued on the three master manipulators.

"I doubt that, but I'm willing to humor you. Pray tell, Rusu, what did I miss?"

"Her." His eyes moved to Zafira, who at the same moment, lifted her right leg and with precision and brutal force, kicked her foot back.

"Christ! *Ty zasraná svině*," Marek cried out as a cavitation pop followed by a sickening crack sounded as the bony surfaces in his knee hit each other when the force of her kick snapped it backward.

All hell broke loose then. Bogdan yanked Zafira from Marek's loosening hold while wringing his gun from his hand with such force that four of his fingers were fractured.

Arian and Andrei shot two of the four men who tried to scramble for cover. The arrival of Izolda and Sabira behind them abruptly ended the others' attempt at escape with a bullet to their chests.

"So, bitch… let's have at it," Vanya taunted Svetlana.

"*Do prdele*, Vanya! Get down," Andrei shouted as he dove at her when the Czech woman raised her gun and pulled the trigger. But he worried for naught. Vanya was already moving, and by the time the bullet buried itself in the wall, she was on Svetlana.

"I'm gonna cut out those two brats inside your belly and feed them to my dogs!" Svetlana spat as she swung the blade in a clockwise spin, only to run into Vanya's savage left hook. The impact was so hard, she dropped hard onto her knees with a soft "oomph."

"No one threatens my children, unborn or not, you fucking bitch!" Vanya sneered as she yanked Svetlana's head up by the hair. "Now, you pay the price." She was barely conscious as Vanya drove her thumb into one eye socket to mash it against her cranial vault. Blind with anger, Vanya tapped into her Krav Maga skills to unleash a devastating kick that suddenly came out of nowhere as her leg swept up, powered by a perfectly timed movement. It exploded at the end of her heel across the front of the redhead's face, splitting her upper lip in two and splintering cartilage through the soft, mushy nasal tissue. "Burn in hell, bitch," Vanya said as Svetlana's eyes rolled up into their sockets. It was light's out... permanently.

"Vanya, get down!"

Andrei's graveled voice echoed through the room with the demand for immediate obedience. She hit the deck as the loud crack of his gun exploding zinged in her ears. Luciano Maranzano's muscled body flung backward against the wall, the gun in his hand clattering to the ground before he managed to pull the trigger. The surprised look on his face was supplemented by the round bullet hole between his eyes.

"Let's see you touch my wife again, you fuckface," Andrei growled as he leaned over to pick Vanya up from the floor. "What about the concept of keeping out of fights and conflict while you are pregnant don't you understand, wife?"

"I tried, honey, but the situation... *hick*... demanded... oh, lordy me... *hick*," she wailed as the tension and hormones clashed, and she burst out in tears. "Don't you d-dare fight with... *sob*... me. I'm... *sob*... p-pregnant."

"Who the fuck would've guessed," Andrei muttered as he carried her outside, murmuring sweet nothings in her ear.

"Now, that just leaves you two lovebirds," Bogdan said, watching Triska fuss over Marek, where he sat on the ground, nursing his knee and broken fingers. "So, Ms. Guzun, it's your call. What do you want me to do with this fuckface?"

"Careful, Bogdan. It's not polite to curse at family, and seeing as he's my brother…"

"Since he's your brother, I'll concede to killing him quickly instead of making him suffer," he offered in an amused tone.

"I second that," Arian growled. "He murdered grandmother and tried to have you killed many times."

"Arian, help me. Vadim has lost a lot of blood. We need to get him to a hospital," Sabira's concerned voice sounded from behind them.

"I'll be okay," Vadim mumbled, but it was clear he was close to passing out. "Stop worrying, Mother. I'm fine," he said as he caught her indecision between going to him and finishing off her enemies.

"Arian, get your brother out of here. Bogdan and I will manage."

Arian didn't need a second invitation, as concern for his brother drove him to act. Like Zafira, he knew Bogdan would never allow anything to happen to her.

"Why kill him at all?" Triska said once they were gone, and Zafira turned to face them. "Why not use us? We've got contacts in places you'll never reach. With our help, the Novaya Volna would rule the world within months instead of years."

"Now see, that's where we differ. I don't believe in rushing anything. Fealties take time to form, and time separates the true followers and loyalists from the deceitful. Something your interference has taught me afresh." Zafira smirked and continued drily, "And don't bother playing on my empathy that you're family," she cut Marek off when he opened his mouth. "If anything, Mother did everyone a favor by giving you away. She must've known you would turn out as selfish and one-dimensional as Father."

"Well, now you're just begging for it," Bogdan said as Marek grabbed the gun with his other hand. Charging forward, Bogdan didn't even check his advance when Marek pulled the trigger, and the bullet penetrated his shoulder. "Time's up, Zafira."

"Do your worst, Bogdan. For what he did to my mother, he deserves nothing better," Zafira retorted with the vision of her mother's mangled body on the coroner's table. Looking back, she now realized the viciousness of her death had spoken of deep hatred and malice. Understandable, but Agata was still his mother. There had been no need to mutilate her body.

Bogdan reacted to the suppressed sadness in Zafira's voice as he reached Marek just as he fired the second shot.

"You heard your sister," he sneered and grabbed his head between his huge hand and with one brutal twist, broke his neck. Adrenaline coursed through his system, activating his sympathetic nervous system. With his heart beating faster, blood got diverted to his muscles and away from his gut. The blade of his K-bar sliced through sinew and muscle when he cut Marek's throat. Flushed with the power of a berserker, Bogdan's muscles bunched.

"Yaaahhh!" His shout echoed over the shocked scream of Triska Cermak as with inhumane force, he twisted his arms and ripped Marek's head right off his body. "*Marcire All 'inferno*, Marek Cermak."

"Oh no, you don't." Zafira stopped Triska from picking up the gun Marek had dropped by pressing the muzzle of her gold-encrusted Glock 9 between her eyes. "I'll make sure your daughter is invited and accepted into our family as one of our own. She deserves to be loved for the wonderful young woman she is, irrespective of how you neglected her all her life. Don't worry, I'll be sure she knows exactly how wanted she was. Oh, one last thing... send my regards to Momma and Poppa, will you? Bye-bye bitch."

The final gunshot sounded with finality through the late afternoon air. The Guzuns were finally free from their nemesis. Life could finally return to normal.

"*Iisus Hristos,* Bogdan! You're bleeding like a stuck pig!" Zafira cried out as Bogdan turned to face her. She didn't watch Triska's lifeless body being flung back with the force of the bullet but rushed to his side. With trembling hands, she yanked off her sweater and tried stemming the blood flowing from the two bullet wounds.

"Stop fussing, woman. It's just flesh wounds. I am fi—" His eyes rolled back in their sockets as with a gruff sigh, his huge body fell backward when he passed out.

"Gmphf, flesh wound indeed," Zafira mumbled as she rushed over to lift his head onto her lap. "You'll probably deny you're dead even when you're pushing up daisies, you hardheaded fool of a wonderful man."

"What was that?"

Zafira didn't blink as his eyes opened and held hers captive.

"What? Oh! That must be the sound reverberating back from the mountains of your big ass body making a dent in the floor. The neighbors must be thinking a nuclear bomb exploded."

"Hmm... not sure what daisies have to do with a bomb exploding, but I'll take your word for that."

He promptly passed out again.

"Typical. He only woke up to pester me, then poof, he's gone."

No one stood witness as the mighty Matriarch brushed her hand over his hair, then leaned in and gently kissed him on the lips. Only the dust particles shimmering in the sun that shone through the wood slats heard the softly whispered words.

"I love you, Bogdan Rusu. I always have. I always will."

Chapter Twenty-Two

Two months later, Senzații de Club, Rose Valley Park, Chisinau, Moldova...

"Now look at that. Master Slayer finally decided to show his face again," Alin Sava said with a pleased grin as Bogdan sat down beside him at the bar. "I began wondering if you had already moved to Russia without saying goodbye."

"I've been recuperating after an incident." Bogdan didn't elaborate. Alin knew better than to ask.

"So, when are you leaving for Russia?"

"I might not be moving permanently after all. I'll definitely be there to help my son get the nursery set up and for the twins' birth, but Moldova is where

I'll stay." He smiled wryly. "That is if my plans work out as I hope."

"Since when do you place your future in the hands of hope? You always go after what you want. Why not this time?"

"It's... complicated."

"Ah... the mighty *Comare*, I imagine. Yeah, she's a tough one. I don't envy you trying to win her over." He glanced toward the dungeon. "That's why you're here? To whip her into admitting how she feels about you?"

"She's here?"

"Strange, isn't it? Coincidently, like you, it's the first time she came back after that scene you had with her. Must be fate."

"I don't believe in celestial nonsense, Alin. Every man is responsible for his own destiny and the path he chooses to make it happen."

"You do you, and I'll do me. I say it's fate that brought you both here tonight. Mark my words. This is going to be the first day of the rest of your lives."

"*Te rog oprește-te,* Alin. You're starting to sound like a telenovela series."

"I'll stop, but just wait and see. I must remember to have my tux dry-cleaned for the wedding."

Bogdan was hard-pressed not to roll his eyes. Instead, he just shook his head, grunted, and walked toward the dungeon. Now was as good a time as any to seal his own fate. After tonight, he would either be the happiest man ever, or he would finally close the chapter on Zafira Guzun once and for all.

It was well past time he moved on with his life.

Zafira had visited him regularly while he was in hospital, but as soon as he was discharged, she stopped checking in on him. Typically, and in usual Bogdan fashion, he didn't pursue her. He had learned his lesson and refused to be rebuffed yet another time. Instead, he had refamiliarized himself with his grand ducal estate to ensure it was well managed should he decide to permanently move to Russia and live with Andrei and Vanya.

He found Zafira perched on the edge of a large wingback chair in the vast reception area of the dungeon that served a double purpose for aftercare. It appeared as if she had been waiting for him. Like the previous time, she wasn't dressed in full kink but rather selected a sheer, black lace dress that enticed as much as it seduced his mind. Underneath, she only wore silver bikini panties that hugged her hips like a lover's hands. Barefoot and with her tresses tumbling like a silky curtain over her shoulders, she was the epitome of femininity. The black lace mask lent a mysteriousness to her appeal that was punctuated by the challenging look in her azure eyes.

The beast inside him reacted to the provocation. With a growl, he was in front of her and yanked her out of the chair. Within moments, he pinned her to the wall with his huge hand clamped around her throat.

"You are teetering on dangerous territory, sub," Master Slayer's dark Dom voice crawled from deep within his soul.

"I laugh in the face of danger, Sir. You, of all people, should know that." Zafira was completely relaxed. Although she was on her toes and struggling to breathe, she didn't claw at the hand tightening around her throat.

Zafira

"There are times when even the most daring should tread with caution. This is one of them."

"It seems here is the only place where the man deep inside is reachable, so what other choice do I have?" Her eyes widened as his fingers threatened to completely cut off her ability to draw enough oxygen into her lungs.

"I came to you with my heart on my sleeve a year ago, Zafira. You chased me off like a lame dog. Ever since you found out I wasn't the bastard you were made to believe I was all those years ago, you've been avoiding me. So, who is the emotionally unattainable one, really? Be honest for once in your fucking life."

"Me! I am the one." She finally clawed at his hand when her chest started burning, and her lips turned blue. "Please, let go, Master Slayer."

"Why? Viktor has been dead for over twenty years. Why did you keep me at a distance all these years?"

"Because I believed you never loved me. I had no reason to doubt my mother. She had never lied to me, and when she told me you had taken the money, something died inside me. When you didn't show up at the wedding, it was all the proof I needed."

"In the meanwhile, I was in jail, where your father and Viktor's father had me incarcerated because I had the audacity to love you."

"I didn't know. You never told me." Tears formed in her eyes. "Why, Bogdan? Why did you never tell me the truth when you returned? I would've believed you. I never loved Viktor. I became fond of him, but I never loved him. When you came back... you could've told me!"

Bogdan stared into her eyes, watching the memories of the past play in their depths like a nightmarish movie reel. The hold on her throat relaxed as he gently moved his fingers in circles to soothe her abused skin.

"You were a very good actress then, Zafira. I believed you were happy, content, and in love with your husband. That day I returned, seeing you with Arian and smiling lovingly at Viktor was like a knife in my heart."

"Why did you stay?"

Zafira

"The look in your eyes. In those years, you hadn't learned to mask your true feelings from me. Why and for what, I didn't know at the time, but it told me that you needed me. I couldn't walk away from you, Zafira. I loved you."

"Loved…" her voice turned sad. "Past tense."

"For love to be sustained, it has to be fed… watered with a daily dose of the same. It's not a one-way street. I am not a young man anymore, and I am tired of going through life alone, hoping that one day you would have the courage to look into your heart and realize you have been living a lie. It's been over forty years. I am done waiting. It's time for me to move on."

"What if I ask you to stay?"

"To what end? More of the same? Be your puppy dog that laps adoringly at your feet? No, thank you." The sigh he released was wrought with acceptance and sadness. "I am a powerful man in my own right, Zafira. You just never realized it, and I was happy to let you be, but I am past that. I have no interest in being controlled and ordered about by you in a professional manner any longer."

"I have come to the same conclusion over the past few weeks myself. I never want you to feel that way ever again." Her fingers trembled as she brushed them over his cheek. "I have missed you so much, Bogdan. Not as my protector or puppy dog lapping at my feet as you say, but as the man who has always held my heart in his hands. That's why I always felt safe, content, and happy. Because you were there." She placed her fingers over his lips to stem the words threatening to fall from them.

"I know it was selfish and wrong. I suppose pride kept me from admitting my feelings. Maybe I wanted you to be the one to force me to acknowledge them. That day you walked away, I was shocked. Even though I chased you away, I never believed you would leave. That was the day I broke down… for the first time and only time in my life, until that night in the dungeon, I cried real tears." She smiled wryly at his look. "Yes, the mighty Comare sobbed her heart out."

"Are you ever going to say it, Zafira?"

Her eyes turned soft and filled with so much devotion, his breath caught in his throat.

Zafira

"I love you, Bogdan Rusu, with all my heart. You fill my soul and awaken my body to euphoric heights I never knew existed." Her eyes filled with tears. "Is there a chance that you could ever forgive me for doubting you?"

Bogdan cupped her chin to stare deep into her eyes. For long moments, he didn't say anything, losing himself in the emotions she didn't hide from him. She was as confident in showing her love for him as she was in every aspect of her life.

"I do love you, Zafira. You captured my heart as a young girl. I tried to move on when I was younger... God knows I did. I never could. No one could ever take the place reserved for you... only you."

"Then it's time, don't you think?"

"I am not interested in a loose relationship, Zafira. You're going to have to be more specific."

"It's time for us to get married and be happy. Become what we were meant to be before life interfered and tore us apart. We belong together, Bogdan. You and me. I want to walk the final journey of my life with you by my side. As my husband... and as my partner in the New Bratva Order."

"I accept, Ms. Guzun. The husband part, at least. The partnership... that's a discussion for a later stage." He ignored her gasp of surprise when he picked her up and headed to the exit. "For now, I'm taking you home. I'm going to need the rest of the night to expunge the hunger you awake in me, and I have no intention of doing it anywhere but in my own bed."

"Only your bed?" Zafira's eyes glimmered with happiness as she wrapped her arms around his neck. "Do you seriously want me to believe you don't have a dungeon at your house?"

His laughter boomed through the vast entrance hall as he strode to the door. "You got me there, love. We'll start in my bedroom, work our way through the dungeon, and see where we end up."

"That's more like it, Master Slayer."

Zafira

Chapter Twenty-Three

Three months later, the luxurious estate of Andrei and Vanya Rusu, Chiverevo, Moscow Oblast, Russia...

"I can't believe the day has finally arrived," Vanya gushed as she faffed over Zafira's hair. "You wasted so much time. The two of you should've been married years ago."

"Hard-headedness runs both ways insofar as Bogdan and my relationship is concerned. Yes,"—she smiled at Vanya's look of reprimand—"I know I'm the one to blame, but it's all in the past. We can't turn back the clock. All we can do is look ahead and make the rest of our life's journey a happy, loving, and lasting one."

"You're right. Hard-headedness runs in the family. All of us had our share of almost losing our chance at happiness because of that. Luckily, love endured and conquered all." Vanya stood back and clapped her hands. "Perfect. You're going to take Bogdan's breath away."

"Good. Knowing how gorgeous he looks in a tux, at least I won't be the only one gawking like a fish on dry land when I first see him."

A knock on the door interrupted their banter.

"Ah, the troops have arrived," Vanya said as Andrei, Vadim, Sabira, Arian, and Izolda piled into the room.

"Now that you're getting married, we felt it's appropriate to make sure nothing is going to get in the way of your happiness," Arian began tentatively.

"I'm a sixty-four-year-old woman, Arian. I don't need my children to give me marital advice," Zafira said with a laugh.

"This isn't about that, but we do have to ask. Does Bogdan know about you being the Shadow Don and the one who is running the Novaya Volna Group?"

"Yes, Arian, he knows."

"And he's happy for you to continue?" The frown on Vadim's face showed his disbelief. Zafira didn't blame him. Ever since Bogdan's return from the U.S., a new man had emerged. Assertive, confident, and much more powerful than she had ever imagined he could be.

"Bogdan is going to be my partner in the Novaya Volna Group. We've already discussed it. I am not prepared to give up my seat as the Shadow Don... not yet. I may never be. It's time the conservative chauvinism of male Bratva leaders comes to an end."

"I'm afraid you might be overreaching, Mother," Arian said with a serious expression. "You might have groups supporting your vision for a modernized future, but a woman being in charge of all? It's not going to happen, and if that's the only reason you offered a partnership to Bogdan, I'm afraid you don't know him as well as we do. The new man is driven, he's powerful, and he's not going to be your henchman or your muscle in your vision."

"*Destul,* Arian! Enough. This is my wedding day. I refuse to allow you to blacken it with predictions of doom."

"It's more than a prediction, Mother. It's a reality. We might support you to a point, but even Vadim, Andrei, and I, in our authority as Bratva leaders, will not bow down to the rule of a woman... even you, our mother."

Zafira felt like she had just been punched in the gut with a ten-pound hammer. She had mostly depended on the support of her own children and their respective Bratva groups. If Vadim was against her rule, so would Sabira, as the leader of the Koval Bratva, be as well. To realize they all sided with the age-old Bratva traditions against her, almost broke her confidence.

Almost... but she was far from ready to give over.

"We shall see. Now, enough of this. Come... it's time to walk your old mother down the aisle. Nothing is going to spoil the wonder and happiness of my wedding day."

Zafira

Sunrise, the following morning, Bogdan's private wing at the Rusu Castle...

"So, are you going to remain a Guzun?" Bogdan kept his tone even, but the way Zafira studied him for long moments warned him he hadn't been successful in hiding his desire to call her all his... and that included her carrying his name. To be reminded for the rest of his life that he had lost her for so long to Viktor Guzun didn't sit well with him. It was time to move on. Leave all the hurt, dissolution, and regrets in the past.

Zafira leaned over to kiss him tenderly. "We started a new life together with this marriage, my love. I believe for us to fully embrace the future and all the happiness it offers; it has to be as a united front. A Rusu unit, so no, like it or not, I'm not going to be a Guzun. From now on, I am Zafira Rusu."

"That just escalated my happiness tenfold, *dragostea mea*."

"Ah, you're lagging behind, *Iubirea mea*. I've been the happiest woman since you returned to Moldova." She hugged him close. "Don't ever do that again, Bogdan. Never leave me for so long. I won't survive the longing, especially now that our love has woven that invisible golden thread through our hearts."

"I'm not going anywhere, *miere*. You're stuck with me now... forever and a day."

"Good, hold that thought. I need to pee."

Bogdan watched her swaying hips as she walked gloriously naked to the en suite bathroom. With a smile, he relaxed against the pillows. Finally, everything had fallen into place. He had the woman he loved by his side. All the hates and regrets are something of the past. A smile rendered victory to his expression as he opened the secret drawer in his bedside table.

"Someone is calling, *miere*," he called out as Zafira's cell phone began buzzing.

"I hope it's not Vanya going into early labor from all the dancing and excitement yesterday," she said as she rushed into the room while wrapping a towel around her. A quick glance at the small screen confirmed it wasn't. She offered an apologetic smile at Bogdan. "Sorry, *Iubirea mea*, I have to take this call."

"Remind whoever it is you're on your honeymoon and that the sun is barely up," he called after her as she rushed out of the room.

Slipping the cell phone from under the cover of the duvet, he lifted his hand to his ear. "I didn't expect to hear from you this soon." Zafira's voice filled his mind. He smiled grimly.

"I believe congratulations are in order, Ms. Guzun, or is it Mrs. Rusu?" His voice was drastically changed by the electronic device attached to the satellite phone.

"It's Rusu, as I'm sure you're aware. Why are you phoning me this early and on the morning after my wedding?" Zafira sounded annoyed but kept her tone respectful.

Bogdan smiled. He had learned deceit from the best. For years, he had watched from the depth of despair and hatred. Now, he had the money, the power, and the following to become what Viktor

Guzun, his father, and grandfather had dreamed of becoming. The all-mighty Shadow Don.

"Remind me, Mrs. Rusu, who is really in charge here? You... or me?"

The silence was thick that followed his words. Bogdan smiled widely. He had played his cards close to the chest for the past forty years, ever since he found out Viktor had known about his father and Zafira's father's plan to have him incarcerated.

"You're the one with the money," she finally said.

Bogdan laughed humorously. It was a pity that Zafira was the one who would pay the price. Not that she stood to lose all that much, except the one thing she had been coveting for the past twenty years... to be what her husband couldn't be... the Shadow Don. Except from day one, there had been a bigger force at play. One who had ducal standing, money, untapped power, and generated fear within the Bratva circles... the *ubiytsa smerti*, the death slayer... Bogdan Rusu.

"It seems you're still under a misconception of our initial agreement, Mrs. Rusu," he said darkly.

Zafira

He got up and stood naked in front of the window, appreciating the golden rays of the early morning sun peeking over the horizon.

"I have more than money. I am the power, and you are my voice. A woman like you is formidable, but that's all you'll ever be. You had the muscle of your newly acquired husband all the years, and that was the only reason you managed to build a following. I recruited the rest and will be the one to ensure their adherence—those of your sons and son-in-law included."

It was a low blow since he knew how upsetting the discussion with her children just before the ceremony had been. He suppressed the desire to give a quarter. Zafira Guzun, now Rusu, had to realize her reign as the Shadow Don, brief as it had been, was over.

"No one in the Bratva world will follow the orders of a woman. You're naive if you believe it would ever come to realization."

"You held me for a fool all these years," Zafira said in a thick voice.

If Bogdan didn't know any better, he would think she was on the verge of tears.

"Ah, not so, Mrs. Rusu. You're the one who had visions of grandeur that were unrealistic. Don't despair. There is a place for you at the top of the organization. As I said, you will be my voice, and that in itself gives you power."

"I worked my ass off to gain power of my own. I don't need you to offer me any. Your voice! That's what you offer me? A voice with no rights, no decision-making, nothing! What power is there in that?"

"That's what's on the table, Zafira. Take it or leave it. You can play a role as the voice of the Shadow Don as a leader, or I can find someone who will. It's your choice. If I were you, I would choose wisely. I'm not the kind of man to let loose ends dangle."

"And if I refuse, I become a loose end."

"You said it. Now... I suggest you trod back to your husband. We don't want him to become suspicious of your doings, now do we?"

Zafira

"Bogdan knows all about the Shadow Don. He helped me set up the Novaya Volna Group. I am not going to exclude him now."

"Oh, I don't want you to. In fact, I want you to offer him the seat as your advisor. Keep him close, and no one will oppose you, but be warned... no one must find out about me. Not even him. You don't wish to become a widow this soon, do you?"

"You touch him, and I will find you. Believe me, Mr. Shadow, no matter where you hide, you won't be safe."

"Ah, true love is such a fragile thing, isn't it? Don't let it make you weak, Mrs. Rusu. I need that steely resolve you're so famous for."

"Fuck off."

Bogdan chuckled as she summarily ended the call. By the time Zafira walked into the room, he was back in bed, pretending to have fallen asleep.

"Hmm, so, who dares interrupt my blissful morning with my beautiful wife," he said in a thick, sleepy voice as she cuddled close to him.

"A mistake that is going to cost me dearly," she said in a quiet voice.

He opened one eye lazily for a moment. "Let's just forget about the world out there for a couple of days, *miere*. We waited years for our time to come. Let's not spoil it with new regrets."

"You're right, *Iubirea mea*," she murmured as she wrapped her arms around him. "Just hold me, Bogdan. Hold me tight and never let go."

"Always, Mrs. Rusu. No one will hurt you. That is my promise to you."

Bogdan was surprised to feel the warm drops of tears falling on his chest. It seems with her love for him came an ability to let go of her emotions. He knew she was angry, but the tears spoke of a vulnerability he never expected to see in her. His heart warmed and swelled at the implication. He had achieved the one thing Viktor Guzun never could.

Zafira Guzun, now Rusu, was becoming the woman she had lost as a young nineteen-year-old girl.

Finally, his life had come full circle... he had the unconditional love of the woman he had yearned for and the prospect of becoming the most powerful being on earth.

The true Shadow Don has risen.

A bright future awaited him after all the years. In the end... patience had paid off.

The End

Linzi Basset

Excerpt: Devious Demand

A brand new series, CLUB DECADENT SKIES, kicking off to the likes of Club Alpha Cove, Club Wicked Cove, Club Devil's Cove, and Castle Sin. So, if you're a fan... this series is for you!

Blurb:

I'm Wick, short for Wicked Witch... yeah, my mother had a weird sense of humor. That our family name is Bitch, and her penchant in those days to be high and drunk, probably aided the name that I've been blessed with. Anyway, as I was about to say, I'm a Private Investigator from Tampa, Miami, and I'm one of the best there is. Why? Because I don't take shit from anyone. Mom should've called me No Shit Bitch... that would've been more appropriate. But I'm digressing again. So, I'm on a job, one that lands me smack bang in the bowel of a super airbus... but

Zafira

if you think it's an airplane with plush seats and top class food, pampering you to your heart's content... you're wrong.

I think I just took on a job I am in no way equipped to handle.

I'm Max DuPont, owner of CyberCo Airlines in Miami. We cater for the rich and famous. Those people who can afford to book an entire luxury airbus for one family. Also... the kind of people who need a secure location to conduct meetings—the kind you don't ask questions about. Money talks and that's the business I'm in. I like to be on top. I thrive on money and power... which is why I am also the primary owner of an exclusive establishment called, Club Decadent Skies.

What I don't need on board the virgin flight of our NY Airbus club, is a snoopy private eye on the job for a man who no sane person should even know exists. She refuses to listen to reason, so, as the Master Owner on board it's my duty to introduce the bratty stowaway to the thrill of what makes people flock to our website—a mile-high experience she wasn't *bound* to forget.

At least bound in my chains of pleasure she would stay alive long enough to change that God awful name of hers.

If you're ready for a one of a kind flight with a suspenseful back storyline that tests Wick and Max's trust and resilience, then this is the series for you.

I am having so much fun *playing* in an exclusive club again, so I hope you'll come along for the flight of a lifetime!

Short Excerpt: Chapter One (Unedited)

It was a damn good thing her mother didn't soft-soap life to Wick growing up—to be clear, that was before she turned alcoholic, and everything went sheepshit. Hell no. Her mother grew up in the time of baby boomers and didn't believe in such bullshit. Nope, to her, and Wick thanked the lord for that every day, it was important that her daughter fought her own battles and didn't wait for a knight on a white horse to save her.

"*A girl in modern times should be her own fucking heroin. Assertive, self-sufficient, and strong so she could withstand a mega shark's attack without being torn to shreds,"* was a famous saying she had drilled into Wick on a daily basis.

Yep, little Wick Bitch wasn't your run of the mill rescue dog with her tail wagging waiting around for approval from any man.

Okay, stop the bus, you say. Lemme explain. Her full name is Wicked Witch, and her surname is Bitch. Don't you dare laugh. Wick had enough of that growing up. She wasn't Christened by that name. As a baby, up to her thirteenth birthday, Wick was known as Willow Carter. Then her dad died, after being stabbed by his latest lover, and left in the street to bleed out like a slaughtered pig. It broke her mother. Why she had changed her daughter's name nobody knew for sure, except perhaps that it was a decision she had made in a drunken and drug induced stupor. It was the worst birthday present any young teenager could ask for… on the same day your mother told you it was your fault your father's eyes strayed. If you weren't born, she would still have had the perfect body, and he wouldn't have lusted after other sluts. It was also the last birthday Wick ever celebrated.

Okay, enough distractions. Back to the story.

Eyes narrowed; Wick studied the man who had just walked through the swivel door of the majestic JCP Corporation building. He moved with confidence, which was to be expected since he was tall and athletic. This was viscerally a man who knew what he was doing, except in her mind's eye, his attitude seemed overdone. The saying, a wolf in sheep's clothing came to mind. She shook her head.

"Look at him," she muttered sotto voce. "Stupid asshole believes he's a primal jaguar, instead he's nothing more than a puppy forging it."

Jax Crowthorne could put any celebrity to shame with his regal frame, rippling gym-trained body, sculpted features, and a neat, well-trimmed beard. Overall, he did things to a woman's ovaries... especially ones who hadn't tasted dick for some time.

"Yeah, that's one hunk of man-steel I wouldn't mind drilling between my legs," she murmured, licking her lips as a vision of slapping flesh and milky discharge momentarily hazed over her thoughts. "As if," she sneered at her reflection in the mirror.

Not that it would ever happen since he was a city rat, and Wick had a natural deflection to the type of male he represented. An established and coveted property developer, he was equally a well-known ladies' man in New York City and Maryland. The kind who didn't commit to one woman but swung his dick from the one to the other, spreading the disease that was him and his chauvinistic prickness all over the States. Why women put up with his rude and obnoxious behavior was beyond Wick.

"But hell, what do I know? I'm nothing but a spinster who doesn't even have a boyfriend or had a cock inside her for over two years." Annoyed and feeling sorry for herself, she took a big bite of the cinnamon coated doughnut in her hand. "Who needs dick stuffed down your throat if you can gorge on delicacies such as this, right?" she mumbled around the buttery sugar pastry in her mouth.

"As if anyone is queueing up outside my door anyway," she sneered at her reflection in the mirror. She'd been called pretty by many. That she was tall, curvy, with pitch black hair styled in a sleek, short Chinese bob, silky marble-like complexion, and Elizabeth Taylor violet-blue eyes, turned many heads—something Wick wouldn't be able to confirm, since she never paid attention. "Yep, that right there," she pointed to the mirror. "That's what I generally look like." She continued in a mutter, "Crumpled, tousled hair, and tired. Gawd, I'm so tired." Except, mostly her messy hair was a sign of her stubborn nature. When she was on a job, there wasn't time to preen and pimp.

Wick started her career as a street cop in the NYPD. With her desire for growth and a natural instinct to think outside the box, she was promoted to the Special Investigation unit within two years. Wick served her time in the country as one of the top level criminal investigators for ten years. Five of which, she led the unit. Then Stephan Jurgen happened...

"Some lessons are harder to learn than others," she said softly as she stuffed the last piece of donut into her mouth. "Needless to say, I won't be making the same mistake again. Yep, no falling in love for this chick ever again. Riding dick on the other hand..."

Her stint with SJ had changed her life and ended her career at the NYPD—by choice. One thing she had learned from her mother was to stand by your beliefs. Not because it was what she had done, but because *she* had done the opposite and became a drunk and a drug addict. Wicked wasn't going to follow in her footsteps. Decision made, she moved to Tampa, Miami, and knowing she had the skills, she started her own private investigation firm, W. Carter Investigators. At least her original name sounded more professional than the one her mother had saddled her with.

"Perhaps it's time for me to change my name back," she muttered. "At least I won't have to watch people laugh when they hear Wicked Witch Bitch."

Her life did a three-sixty turn three years ago. Now, she was riding the wave of success after working long, hard hours the first year she had started. With fifteen permanent staff members, of which ten were investigators, the business was booming. They were busy... because they were good.

"Mom should've called me No Shit Bitch," she mumbled while chewing and swallowing the final mouthful of coffee. "Oh, c'mon Crowthorne, get a move on," she complained as she shifted in the seat. "I've got leg cramps from waiting for you this long."

When she had accepted the job, she had no idea it would bring her back to her old hometown. Not that she had spent any time looking around or visiting old hangouts since her arrival. There hadn't been time. Her client had a time limit on this job, and Wick never failed to deliver.

"This alphahole is too much of a busybody to let me have any fun," she complained as she started the car when the black Bugatti finally pulled away from the curb. "Running around all over town from sunrise to sunset, and now... ah shit, he's heading to the airport." She slammed her palm against the steering wheel. "I'm not losing this motherfucker. Tonight, I'm gonna hit the jackpot. One way or the other I'm going to get the proof my client needs that he's a corrupt businessman." She pointed to the roof of the rental. "Not even a stint up there is going to save you, asshole. I'll be on the same plane as you, even if I have to stowaway."

Wick cringed at her own words. She always walked the straight and narrow path. Inherently, she believed in the law and strived to conduct her business within those parameters. "You better not be fucking stringing me along, Jax Crowthorne." Wick might be a stickler for doing what was right, but at the same time, she didn't shy away from challenges or letting her hair loose and doing something wild and dangerous. If it meant she'd crack a case, all the more reason to step outside the red line now and then.

"This isn't my first rodeo, just so you know, buster. I've done loads of stake outs. I'm gonna be up your ass the whole time and you won't even feel it."

It wasn't a vain boast. It was the truth. Wick had learned during her mother's stints of drowning her sorrows in booze and snorting coke, to melt into the walls, so to speak, to avoid the violent spells that were sparked by the narcotics in her system.

"Ah, shit, I was right. He is going to the airport." She eased her foot off the gas pedal and allowed the distance between the rental sedan and the super sport's car to stretch. "Not the terminal though. Freaking asshat! You have to make things difficult, don't you," she muttered as he passed through a security gate with no more than a wave at the guard who opened the boom for him. "No way I'm getting through there."

Parking the car in the parking lot, she realized it was packed with luxury sedans, SUVs, and limousines. With her eyes peeled on the black Bugatti, she followed its route until it stopped next to a sleek, pitch black airbus. He ascended the stairs and stood staring out toward the sky for long moments before disappearing from view.

"Wow," she said and stared in awe. "What a gorgeous plane." A thin golden thread weaved across the side of the plane to end on the rudder wing with what appeared to be a gold tiger's eye. It looked sleek, helluva expensive, but dark and dangerous at the same time. Signed in decorative cursive, the letters CDS were prominent on the side of the cockpit.

"What the flying fuck do we have here?" Getting out of the car, and hunching over, she ran closer to the ten foot electric fence to peek around, looking for a way to get past the guard. "I have to get inside that plane."

As luck would have it, she noticed a group of servers, dressed in white and black, getting out of a van and walking toward the gate. Waiting until they were close, she quickly circled until she was behind them and quietly slipped into the queue. She might not be as crisp as they were but at least her black jogging pants and white T-shirt allowed her to blend in.

"You're late. You know how Master M feels about tardiness," the guard's voice was reproachful. "Don't bother with excuses," he cut short the chorus that erupted from the group. "Just get on board before he fires the lot of you."

Now that was a stroke of genius," she said sotto voce as she broke into a run alongside the group toward the plane who became more impressive the closer they got. Luckily, they were all in too much of a hurry to pay attention to a stowaway trailing them up the stairs and into the galley of the plane. Releasing a sigh of relief, she looked around. She was just about to grab a white chef's overcoat when she was brought to an abrupt halt by a grip of steel closing around her throat.

"What the fuck!? Let me go," she snapped as she attempted to free herself. Instead, she was bulldozed down a short hallway, spun around and slammed against the wall with the same hand clamped around her throat.

"That is a very good question, little witch. Who are you and what the fuck are you doing on this plane?"

So, don't miss out. Preorder DEVIOUS DEMAND book 1 now. Releasing June 25th.

Books by Linzi Basset

Louisiana Daddies
Covert Daddy – Prequel
Black Ops Daddy – Book 1
Radical Daddy – Book 2
Dominant Daddy – Book 3
Marauding Daddies – Book 4

Grace's Initiation
The Interview – Prequel
S is for Safeword – Book 1

The Guzun Trilogy
Vadim – Book 1
Vanya – Book 2
Arian – Book 3
Andrei – Book 4
Zafira – Book 5

Decadent Sins Series
Dominant Nature – Book 1
Dominant Desire – Book 2
Dominant Demand – Book 3
Dominant Thrills – Book 4
Dominant Mercy – Book 5

Castle Sin Series
Hunter - Prequel
Stone – Book 1
Hawk – Book 2
Kane – Book 3
Ace – Book 4

Linzi Basset

Parker – Book 5
Zeke – Book 6
Shane – Book 7
Danton – Book 8
Billy & Mongo – Book 9
Peyton – Book 10

Club Devil's Cove Series
His Devil's Desire – Book 1
His Devil's Heat – Book 2
His Devil's Wish – Book 3
His Devil's Mercy – Book 4
His Devil's Chains – Book 5
His Devil's Fire – Book 6
Her Devil's Kiss – Book 7
His Devil's Rage – Book 8
The Devil's Christmas – Book 9
The Devilish Santa – Book 10

Club Wicked Cove Series
Desperation: Ceejay's Absolution–Book 1
Desperation: Colt's Acquittal – Book 2
Exploration: Nolan's Regret – Book 3
Merciful: Seth's Revenge – Book 4
Claimed: Parnell's Gift – Book 5
Decadent: Kent's Desire – Book 6
Wicked and Fearless – Box Set, Books 1 – 3
Wicked and Deadly – Box Set, Books 4 - 6

Club Alpha Cove Series
His FBI Sub – Book 1

Zafira

His Ice Baby Sub – Book 2
His Vanilla Sub – Book 3
His Fiery Sub – Book 4
His Sassy Sub – Book 5
Their Bold Sub – Book 6
His Brazen Sub – Book 7
His Defiant Sub – Book 8
His Forever Sub – Book 9
His Cherished Sub – Book 10
For Amy – Their Beloved Sub – Book 11

The Bleeding Souls Trilogy
Kiss the Devil - Prequel

The Stiletto PI Series
Fierce Paxton – Book 1
Fiery Jordan – Book 2

Billionaire Bad Boys Romance
Road Trip
Rogue Cowboy

Dark Desire Novels
Enforcer – Book 1

Their Sub Novella Series
No Option – Book 1
Done For – Book 2
For This – Book 3
Their Sub Series Boxset

Linzi Basset

Their Command Series
Say Yes – Book 1
Say Please – Book 2
Say Now – Book 3
Their Command Series Boxset

Romance Suspense

Just Us Series
Just a Kiss – Book 1

The Bride Series
Claimed Bride – Book 1
Captured Bride – Book 2
Chosen Bride – Book 3
Charmed Bride – Book 4

Caught Series
Caught in Between
Caught in His Web

The Tycoon Series
The Tycoon and His Honey Pot
The Tycoon's Blondie
The Tycoon's Mechanic

Standalone Titles
Her Prada Cowboy
Never Leave Me, Baby

Zafira

Now is Our Time
The Wildcat that Tamed the Tycoon
The Poet's Lover
Sarah: The Life of Me
Axle's Darkness

Naughty Christmas Stories
Her Santa Dom
Master Santa
Snowflake's Spanking

Box sets
A Santa to Love – with Isabel James
Christmas Delights – with Isabel James
Unwrapped Hearts – with Isabel James

Books written as Kimila Taylor
Paranormal Books
Guardian's Spell
Zaluc's Mate
Slade: Blood Moon
Azriel: Rebel Angel

Books Co-Written as Isabel James

Zane Gordon Novels
Truth Untold

The Crow's Nest
A journey of discovery on the White Pearl

Linzi Basset

Christmas Novellas
Santa's Kiss
Santa's Whip
Mistletoe Bride

Poetry Bundle by Linzi Basset & James Calderaro
Love Unbound - Poems of the Heart

Zafira

About the Author

"Isn't it a universal truth that it's our singular experiences and passion, for whatever thing or things, which molds us all into the individuals we become? Whether it's hidden in the depths of our soul or exposed for all to see?"

Linzi Basset is a South African born animal rights supporter with a poet's heart, and she is also a bestselling fiction writer of suspense-filled romance erotica books; who as the latter, refuses to be bound to any one sub-genre. She prefers instead to stretch herself as a storyteller which has resulted in her researching and writing historical and even paranormal themed works.

Her initial offering: Club Alpha Cove, a BDSM club suspense series released back in 2015, and catapulted her into International Bestseller status. Labelling her as prolific is a gross understatement as just a few short years later she has now been published over a hundred times; a total which includes the other published works of her alter ego: Isabel James who co-authors and alternative penname, Kimila Taylor.

"I write from the inside out. My stories are both inside me and a part of me, so it can be either pleasurable to release them or painful to carve them out. I live every moment of every story I write. So, if you're looking for spicy and suspenseful, I'm your girl ... woman ... writer ... you know what I mean!"

Linzi believes that by telling stories in her own voice, she can better share with her readers the essence of her being: her passionate nature; her motivations; and her wildest fantasies. She feels every touch as she writes, every kiss, every harsh word uttered, and this to her is the key to a never-ending love of writing.

Ultimately, all books by Linzi Basset are about passion. To her, passion is the driving force of all emotion; whether it be lust, desire, hate, trust, or love. This is the underlying message contained in her books. Her advice: "Believe in the passions driving your desires; live them; enjoy them; and allow them to bring you happiness."

Find out more here:
https://www.linzibassetauthor.com/

Stalk Linzi Basset

If you'd like to look me up, please follow any of these links.

While you're enjoying some of my articles, interviews, and poems on my website, why not subscribe to my Newsletter and be the first to know about new releases and win free books? You will also receive a free eBook copy of The Interview and The Poet's Lover.

Go to my website, www.linzibassetauthor.com, and while you're there, subscribe to her newsletter: https://www.linzibassetauthor.com/subscribe

Find all my social links and follow me here:
https://linktr.ee/LinziBasset

Don't forget to join my fan group, Linzi's Reading Nook, for loads of fun!

Don't be shy, pay me a visit, anytime!

Milton Keynes UK
Ingram Content Group UK Ltd.
UKHW022343050624
443649UK00019BA/1190

9 798224 033744